HEART OF STONE

Khargals of Duras

REGINE ABEL

Copyright © 2019

ALL RIGHTS RESERVED

This book uses mature language and explicit sexual content. It is not intended for anyone under the age of 18.

This book is a work of fiction freely inspired by the Ant and the Grasshopper fable. Names, characters, places, and incidents either are products of the author's imagination or are used fictitiously. Any resemblance to actual persons, living or dead, events, or locales is entirely coincidental.

INTRODUCTION

A thousand years ago, a Khargal scouting party left Duras, only to crash on a planet called Earth.

Injured and outnumbered, the stranded Khargals hid among stone effigies and observed the slow evolution of the planet's primitive inhabitants. With no means of returning to Duras, they watched from their shadowy perches and faded into legend, becoming the mythical gargoyles.

Until today. Long after any hope for rescue had died, the distress signal has finally been answered.

It's time to go home.

HEART OF STONE

Her winged savior was no angel.

When death nearly claims Brianna at the tender age of eight, a being that shouldn't exist saves her. Twenty years later, she becomes an architectural engineer specializing in historic buildings, still searching for evidence that the one who saved her—the one who haunts her increasingly wild dreams—truly exists. When a mystery man hires her for a major project in the catacombs of an old church turned exclusive, gothic night-club, Brianna believes she may have her chance at long last.

Alkor has grown weary of this era. Forced to hide in plain sight, forbidden from ever claiming the only woman who ever stirred his mating instincts, he considers going back into hibernation rather than pining for her from afar. But the sudden activation of the beacon changes everything. Rescue is coming at last. With his only means of reaching the rendezvous point trapped in the catacombs, Alkor hires

Brianna to help recover his treasure. However, his lost sigil isn't the only thing he intends to take back home with him.

Time is running out, and the evil forces conspiring to capture him will stop at nothing to achieve their goal, even using Brianna. Did Alkor save his true mate only to lose her now that they might have a chance at a future together?

CONTENTS

DEDICATION

To the other six amazing authors who shared this collaborative adventure with me. Thanks for all the laughs, the sprints, the jinxes, and keeping me awake long past my bedtime with your silly banter. A special thanks to Stephanie West for your endless optimist, amazing cheerleading skills, and keeping us all so organized. Heart of Stone made it in large part thanks to you. You were my rock.

To my wonderful beta readers, you ladies always go above and beyond. Thank you for your continued support and friendship. Consider yourselves hugged and wrapped in my virtual wings!

ALKOR

The humans hopped, wiggled, and writhed on the dance floor to the thumping sound of the bass. Most of them wore black, dark reds, and purple, each one embracing the temporary illusion of belonging to the Underworld. Goths, Punk-rock, cosplaying witches, warlocks, demons, and the occasional fallen angel, the patrons rivaled each other in the realism of their respective costumes. And yet, none could ever equal or surpass mine.

Leaning on the railing of the balcony of my private booth, I flexed my wings, their leathery texture brushing against my back. Many of the patrons peered at me from below or from the VIP lounges on each side of my private box which occupied the entire back wall. The dim lights inside The Darkest Hour, the most exclusive themed club in downtown Montreal —although we usually referred to it as a Goth club—allowed me to hide that my horns and wings weren't prosthetics or part of a costume, but integral parts of my body.

So many rumors and wild speculations had been spread

about Alkor Drayvus, the mysterious owner of The Darkest Hour. I neither denied nor confirmed any of them. Those who had gotten close enough to talk to me, or even touch me, assumed I was one of those 'eccentric' people who had gone hardcore with transforming their appearance like Lizardman, Alien Man, or Zombie Boy. That belief served my purpose, allowing me to show my true self, although it wouldn't pass any up-close examination. My horns, facial bones, or tail could be explained by implants. But I'd never get away with intense scrutiny of my wings.

I envied the casual abandon with which the patrons danced, drank, and mingled, some finding dark corners to explore other types of pleasures. While fairly tolerant with patrons heavily groping and petting each other, I didn't allow things to get too steamy as some had tried in the past, especially the vampire wannabes. After all, I'd built this club in an old gothic church right in the heart of downtown Montreal. Such lewd behavior would be unbecoming in a formerly holy place.

After forty-four years of hibernation, followed by five years of aimless wandering, The Darkest Hour had been an opportunity to let me interact with humans again, while still hiding in plain sight. But nine years of running the successful club was losing its appeal. Although surrounded by hundreds of people, I'd never felt so alone. A haunting face with bright blue eyes and silky, golden-brown hair flashed before my mind's eye. I chased it away along with the ache that it always stirred in my heart. Yes, hibernation would be good, if only to spare me the torture of longing for the forbidden. If I turned my heart and body to stone in the deep sleep of *duramna*, I could reawaken at the end of her human lifespan. Why subject myself to useless pain and temptation?

When she reappeared in my life nine years ago as a fully-grown woman, for the first time, she stirred my mating instincts. Thoughts of her have been plaguing me ever since.

The door of my private balcony opening startled me. Looking over my shoulder, I watched Lana strut her way in, wearing a painted on dress which reminded me of Morticia Addams' black dress.

So much for me being an elite warrior.

I'd be shamed if my battalion knew that a doll-like, human female had so easily gotten the drop on me. But then, I hadn't made use of my warrior skills in a couple of centuries now.

"How's my favorite brooding man?" Lana asked, flicking the tip of one of my wing spurs; an annoying habit she had picked up in the past couple of years.

"Broodier than ever," I said, resting my elbow on the balcony railing. "And I'm not a man."

"Fine, male gargoyle" she said with a shrug.

"It's not gargoyle, it's Khargal," I insisted, wondering why I was being so difficult.

"Well, someone woke up on the wrong side of his pedestal," Lana said, a teasing glimmer in her eyes.

"Indeed. I... I'm losing interest in this era," I admitted, giving her an apologetic look.

Lana was the firstborn child of the Dalghren heir. For generations, the oldest child of that bloodline became my human contact, allowing me to function in a world where I didn't belong; a burden they voluntarily accepted. Lana was a sister to me, although she often acted more like my mother. She'd gone out of her way to make this era palatable for me.

For nine, almost ten years now, she'd nearly succeeded. If not for my unattainable mate, I might actually have enjoyed this era and its booming technological advances.

"You can't for at least another four months," she said, trying to hide the sadness in her eyes. "You promised to take my son on a flight over the St. Lawrence River for his ninth birthday."

I nodded, smiling fondly at the thought of the little imp, his mother's spitting image with his undisciplined mess of red hair and the swarm of freckles stamped all over his face—even on the lips. Lana had made me his godfather.

To this day, the memory of the priest presiding over little Tommen's christening eyeing me suspiciously still had me in knots. Although I'd cut off my horns, and hidden the stumps under my hair, my facial bones resembling tiny ivory horns along my jawline, had somewhat given away my 'other-worldly' nature. I'd retracted my wings and tucked my tail into my pants. At the time, my perception filter, the camouflage technology that allowed me to take on any appearance I wished, had been defective. As I hadn't managed to repair it in time, I'd opted not to use it. When a sudden itch had made my tail jerk alongside my legs, looking like a writhing snake, the priest's eyes had all but popped out of his head. I'd expected him to start throwing holy water at me while chanting exorcism incantations.

"Of course, I will," I said, pulling on a strand of her long, reddish hair. "A promise is a promise."

"Ow!" she said, swatting my hand with false outrage, scrunching her pretty face. "If you want to pull a woman's hair, how about you give that Sandy what she wants, and get her off my back?"

I rolled my eyes in disbelief. "Seriously? Again?" I asked.

"She's pretty damn desperate to get you back in the sack. You must have skills, wing-man," she said, making a disgusted face.

That made me chuckle. I could see how hearing of my sexual performance would make her cringe. What sister would want to hear other women fawn over her brother's prowess in bed? I'd kept such encounters to an extreme minimum, with Sandy being my second one-night stand in the nine years since my reawakening. She didn't want any type of commitment from me or to even have any kind of conversation with me. I was merely an exotic trophy she liked having on her bedpost, and an unusual cock she had liked getting pounded by, propped against the back wall of my private booth.

But I had no interest in being Sandy's sex toy, or any other female's for that matter. Her ego would eventually recover since her heart certainly wasn't involved. In truth, my kind rarely indulged in such intimacy for fun, our libido remaining rather dormant until we found the person we wanted to mate with. Moments of intense loneliness, and hopeless longing for something I could never have, had driven me to seek comfort in the wrong places. Both times had fulfilled my need for physical closeness, but not the gaping hole in my heart and soul.

"Tell Sandy to find herself a new stallion. As agreed, it was a one-time deal. I'm happy to go tell her myself," I added, when Lana rolled her eyes.

"Hell no, wing-boy! Your diplomatic skills are appalling," Lana exclaimed. "I've got this. Anyway, we have a new patron Sandy will probably chase after. He has everyone staring in awe."

"Unicorn boy?" I asked.

She burst out laughing. "Actually, he's a dragon wannabe. That's his first horn implant. His surgeon wouldn't graft another one before he saw how he reacted to the first one."

I shook my head, not understanding these strange human compulsions to change their nature. But I wouldn't complain; they provided me with the cover I needed to have a semblance of a normal life.

"But getting you to do the horizontal dance with Sandy isn't why I came to pester you," Lana said, becoming serious again. "I'm getting a lot of requests for opening another Goth club, but this time in Helsinki."

"There are no Khargals there," I countered, frowning slightly.

"I know, but don't forget that 99.9% of your clientele isn't Khargal," Lana said with a shrug. "The concept really appeals to people, especially now that you've relaxed the rules… in other locations."

I harrumphed, which made Lana smile mockingly at me. I was a bit of a stickler for rules and protocols. It bothered me that every Goth club in the chain I had now established wasn't built in an abandoned church, and that the customers weren't held to the strict dress code demanded here at The Darkest Hour. But some of the other locations, such as the Evensong in New York, had a more laidback clientele. A single Khargal frequently mingled with humans there—my old friend Frelinray.

"With the Fins having only five hours of daylight during a

part of winter, it's the perfect setting for people with vampire fetishes," Lana said, matter-of-factly.

"And what happens when summer comes rolling in and then it switches to only five hours of nighttime a day?" I asked.

"Then the vampire customers can cover themselves in pixie dust so they can sparkle in the sun," Lana deadpanned.

I laughed out loud and shook my head again. "Well, you're the one managing all this stuff. So if you want to open one there, go right ahead. Just tell me where to sign."

"I wanted to give you the heads up since I just hung up with the potential partner over there," Lana said, cautiously. "It's worth putting the business proposal together to see if it's a viable option."

I nodded, my mind wandering, thinking of the interesting opportunities a trip to Finland would grant me. With the long hours of darkness, I could fly around more frequently with fewer risks of being spotted, at least for part of the year. Settling down in downtown Montreal had not been the smartest idea on that front. At least, a short drive to the South Shore brought me to wide open fields where I could take flight in relative security.

A sudden wave of dizziness washed over me, and an odd tingling at the base of my neck spread over my scalp. My synapses all seemed to fire at the same time as a long-forgotten sensation buzzed through my brain.

"No *gracking* way!" I whispered, leaning on the railing for support.

"Al, are you okay?" Lana asked, a worried expression on her face.

"It activated," I breathed out. "My *gracking* sigil just activated."

"Your sigil?" Lana asked, hesitantly. "As in your lost homing device?"

"It's not lost," I said absent-mindedly, my mind reeling. "It's buried in the rubble in the catacombs underneath us. We need to get it back. Quickly!"

I fisted my hair, looking at the dancing crowd below, unseeing. A thousand years… One thousand *gracking* years my brothers and I had been stranded on this planet after our ship had crashed. Why was the rescue mission finally coming now? How was it even possible with our beacon destroyed? Had one of the surviving Khargals built a new one? Did our original one, lost in orbit around the planet, finally fall back to Earth?

But those questions were of little importance. All that mattered was that our people had finally received our distress signal and would be coming to rescue us. Except, I needed my sigil not only to get the location, the time, and date of our pickup, but also because it served as the teleport device they would lock onto in order to transport me to the ship.

"Based on previous rescues, the ship will give us a 24-hour window for the pick-up which will take place two to four weeks from now, considering the required travel time from Duras," I said, my heart beating harder than the bass thumping beneath my feet. "I need to retrieve my sigil within the week so that I have enough time to make it to the rendezvous point."

"Well, it's too late tonight," Lana said, pensively, "I will have some people come over first thing in the morning to inspect the catacombs. But Al, one week…"

"Make it happen, Lana," I said in a tone that brooked no argument. "I know exactly where I hid the sigil before the collapse. They only need to clear a path."

"Fair enough, but we'll need a construction permit, and…"

The look on my face must have said it all. Lana sighed heavily, not bothering to list the countless—very valid—arguments as to why this timeline would prove challenging.

I never thought we'd be rescued, or I would have had the catacombs cleared years ago. A botched underground pipe and sewage job along the road outside the church had caused the collapse of sections of the catacombs of the already old building. I'd hidden my sigil within it during the mid-1800s and stood watch over the building as one of the gargoyles adorning its roof. With the population's waning interest in religion and the rising costs of operating the building, the church was eventually put up for sale in the late 1900s. Through some major wheeling and dealing, Lana's father had managed to prevent the church from being classified a historical building, although with some heavy promises that it wouldn't be torn down or heavily modified to the point of making it unrecognizable.

I'd had no need or desire to defile the building nor to turn it into another business or apartment complex. I only required a safe place to keep my sigil and the few remaining pieces of Khargal equipment and technology I still possessed, as well as a place I could hibernate in stone form without anyone questioning my presence.

"Fine, let me see what I can do," Lana said. "I guess that means Tommen doesn't get to have his gargoyle flight."

"I'll take him next weekend," I said with a conciliatory smile. "Call it an early birthday gift."

Lana smiled back, but I didn't miss the sadness in her eyes. I would miss her as much as I knew she'd miss me.

"I'll hold you to it, stony-boy," Lana said, flicking my right wing spur. "Time to make some emergency phone calls."

Turning on her heels, she headed towards the exit of my private booth.

"Lana," I called out as she reached for the door. She looked at me over her shoulder. "Thank you."

She smiled, winked, and then walked out.

❧ 2 ☙

BRIANNA

Heart pounding, I tried to keep a stoic face while Lana Dalghren ushered me inside The Darkest Hour. When my firm received her message this morning, I all but begged my boss to let me take on this project. I'd been trying for years to get close to the mysterious owner of the exclusive club, but to no avail. Others before me had been allowed to have private conversations with him. Not me. Never me. For some reason, I appeared to have been blacklisted. And yet, I'd never acted demanding or aggressive, unlike some of the people who actually got to meet him.

The last time I'd tried, two years ago, Lana had been polite but firm in stating that Mr. Drayvus had no desire to speak to me, now or ever. That had stung. No, that had broken my heart. What had I done to be so brutally rejected? Rather than deterring me, it further fueled my theory that he might be the one I'd been looking for and that he feared a potential reunion.

After all this time, I wondered if Lana would recognize

me, and if that would prompt her to turn me away. Her heavy stare confirmed she did remember me, but showing her my business card sufficed to gain me entry. My eyes flicked around the place, taking it in for the first time properly lit and devoid of the masses of bodies that usually swarmed it. The silence felt eerie, our footsteps echoing loudly in the mostly empty former church.

A few waiters ran around, setting up the tables for the restaurant service which would begin a couple of hours from now and go until 8:00 P.M. when the place would turn into a nightclub again.

"This way, Ms. Brent," Lana said, leading me towards a thick door at the back. "Alkor wants to expand the club with thematic rooms in the old catacombs. Unfortunately, you might recall the mess that occurred a few years back which caused part of them to collapse?"

I nodded, remembering all too well the lawsuits that had ensued for the gross negligence which could have cost lives.

"Good," Lana continued as she opened the massive door, revealing a large stone staircase leading into the catacombs. She began her descent, and I followed in her wake. "When my boss sets his mind on something, he wants it yesterday. In this instance, he actually *needs* the first room opened up within the week for a very special event. For now, you do not have to worry about having a full design of the rooms and layouts, we just need to help make sure the construction workers remove the rubble in that first room without jeopardizing the integrity of the building."

"Yes, of course. However, we need permits—"

"We will pay whatever extras are required to expedite the process," Lana interrupted. "I understand we can get an urgent one delivered in twenty-four hours. Money is not going to be an issue, as long as you get that room opened up within seven days."

"All right," I said as we reached the basement.

"You are the third firm I've met this morning about this project," Lana said, turning to face me. "The first one stated in no uncertain terms they couldn't deliver within our time frame. The second said they would get back to us with a firm commitment by 14:00 today. Would you be able to do the same?"

"Based on the schematics you sent with your message last night, and the inspection reports attached, unless something has radically changed since they were drafted, I see no reason we can't deliver as per your request," I said, confident about my assessment. I wanted this job, really badly, but not so much as to risk my career on false promises. "Naturally, it will cost you substantially more than if we were trying to offer you a competitive price with a laxer timeline. But if, as you say, money isn't an issue, then by the time I finish looking at the place, I should be able to confirm that we can indeed do this for you."

"Good answer," Lana said, with a broad smile.

I smiled back, instantly liking her. Even during my previous encounters with her, she'd always been a polite, classy lady. Peering around the rectangular room made of dark, beige stone in which we had landed, I smiled at the familiar feeling of being transported back in time whenever I visited old churches. The dusty, musty scent of closed off places greeted us as we entered the room which had four hallways branching off, two on the left and right sides, and a longer corridor straight ahead that was almost completely blocked off by rubble, Lana indicated for me to proceed to the second passage on the right. Gravelly stones crunched beneath my feet as we walked on the floor made-up of the same stones as those used in the walls.

To my relief, despite the collapse, the structure seemed as sound as the post-incident reports had stated. Up ahead, I could see the first signs of rubble obstructing the room. As we approached the opening, Lana's phone went off. She picked it up and listened for a few seconds.

"Dammit," she cussed. "Fine, I'm coming." Lana hung up then turned to me. "I must go handle something upstairs. I'll be back in a minute. The room is straight ahead. This is a dead end, so you cannot get lost."

"No problem. I'll be fine," I said, smiling reassuringly.

It actually suited me not to have someone hovering over my shoulder while I tried to get work done. Lana nodded then backtracked her steps to the upper floor. I crossed the rest of the way to the room. No doors closed it off, only a huge arched doorway with a big pair of sconces illuminating the entrance. Although they looked like ancient torches, they were actually electric wall lamps.

Stepping inside the room, my heart nearly stopped. On the left side, on an oddly placed pedestal, a massive, stone gargoyle stared into the room. I yelped in surprise and then my brain froze.

I knew this face. The face that had haunted my dreams for the past twenty years.

I found you!

Knees trembling, I approached him with wobbly steps.

Not him, it.

Who would have carved such a large, life-like replica of

the man… creature that had saved me so many years ago? From the first time I'd heard a description of Alkor Drayvus, I'd wondered if he could be him. I'd never been able to get a good look at him, and he never allowed anyone to get a proper picture of him. But even from a distance, he appeared too young to be the one who had saved me from drowning… unless he hadn't aged a day.

I raised a trembling hand to the face of the gargoyle. Cold stone met my touch, the texture oddly soft and polished. My fingers roamed over its eyes, its nose, and strangely human lips, then back up to the short, pointy horns that adorned its head almost like a crown. They reminded me of the ones from those aliens in Star Wars—like that Darth Maul guy. It had to be the most handsome gargoyle I'd ever seen, with almost human features. Hands clasping the edge of the perch upon which it crouched, its muscular chest and bulging arms had me drooling. In the years since Alkor Drayvus had opened The Darkest Hour, he had starred in many of my naughtiest nighttime fantasies, where he looked exactly like this gargoyle.

With a will of their own, my palms leisurely explored his broad chest. The sculptor's attention to detail—down to the nipples on the statue—just blew my mind. My fingers were tracing the lines of his eight-pack when movement at the edge of my vision startled me. I glanced down between his arms at his crotch and stared at a strange bulge—too conveniently placed—that I hadn't noticed before. Looking back up at his face… rather *its* face, I recoiled slightly. His lips seemed to form a bit of a sneer, with the tips of sharp fangs protruding. I didn't recall seeing those either earlier. Were my eyes playing tricks on me?

You were too busy drooling over those sexy muscles.

I lifted my hand back to his face and ran my thumb over his lips. For some irrational reason, I pressed the pad of my thumb on the tip of his fang. It proved far sharper than I'd expected, nicking me. With a slight hiss, I pulled my hand away and sucked the pearl of blood seeping from it. Looking back down, my jaw dropped.

That bulge wasn't THAT big seconds ago. I'm sure of it!

But stone didn't shift like that. Or was it stone? Ever the 'act first, think later' kind of girl, I reached for his... its crotch and squeezed the bulge.

Stone.

Cold, hard, and unyielding beneath my touch, my imagination was clearly running wild.

"What the hell are you doing?" Lana asked, the sound of her—very upset—voice making me squeal in surprise.

I yanked my hand away from the gargoyle's groin and spun around to look at her. I didn't need a mirror to imagine the guilty and mortified expression plastered on my face. How did you explain to a potential client that you'd been molesting a statue because you thought it had grown a boner?

"I'm sorry," I said, my cheeks burning with humiliation. "I shouldn't have touched the statue. It's just such an incredibly realistic piece. And... the model greatly resembles someone I knew before."

She narrowed her eyes at me. "Someone you knew?"

"It's... Well, I didn't *know* the person, but... Do you know who the model was for this statue? His face looks exactly like the man who saved my life twenty years ago. I've been looking for him ever since to thank him. So seeing his face on that statue threw me for a loop."

A strange expression crossed her features. In that instant, I believed she knew who the model was, or maybe even the man. I wouldn't press my luck just now, but I believed that man was somehow related to her boss.

"I'm sorry, the statue came with the building," Lana said. "So, about the work…?"

"Right," I said, snapping out of my daze, "I will need about thirty minutes, then I will be able to give you my answer."

"Perfect."

ALKOR

My blood boiled with a rabid hunger. Had Lana not entered the room when she had, I'd have emerged from my stone form, thrown the foolish engineer onto the floor, and ravished her right there and then. My cock throbbed with unsated need. It wasn't bad enough that the moment I saw her my mating glands went into overdrive; she had to touch me, too. How could Lana have let her in? Surely she'd recognized the female?

Brianna had blossomed into a beautiful woman. Twenty years ago, during one of my nighttime flights, I'd witnessed a drunk driver losing control of his vehicle and ramming into another car. The vehicle had barrel-rolled before falling into the river. Brianna's mother had been killed instantly. Her father had been injured and unconscious, although he did come around shortly thereafter. Brianna had been uninjured but trapped in the back seat while their vehicle sank. I'd pulled them both out, leaving the mother since she was beyond help. The little girl had watched me with bulging eyes, from both shock and disbelief. Being on the smaller side, I'd assumed her to be about six years old but, according to the news in the following days, she'd been eight.

For years afterwards, I'd thought she would have forgotten about the strange being that had flown her and her father back to safety before disappearing into the night. Or perhaps she would have believed that shock had made her invent a mythical figure to explain how they had survived. But when she showed up at The Darkest Hour, soon after its opening nearly ten years ago, I realized she remembered and was committed to tracking me down.

Then, like now, the instant she had come within range, my mating instincts had awakened, causing my mating glands to become active. Only a female meant to be a Khargal's life mate could trigger such a response. When I rescued her, twenty years ago, I had no idea that I was saving my *Hondassa*. As much as I ached to claim her now, to put an end to my loneliness, I'd done everything in my power to keep her at arm's length. The Prime Directive dictated we keep our existence secret from humans. Anyway, what kind of life would I be able to offer her or our potential offspring? They'd be forever condemned to living in hiding with me, as I'd had to do for the past thousand years.

But the sigils becoming active changed everything.

Remaining still on my pedestal, willing my hard-on to subside, proved a torture of Spanish Inquisition proportion. The feel of her hand on my crotch lingered while I watched her inspecting the room, taking measurements, and jotting down notes. As upset as Lana had been, she now cast mocking glances at me whenever Brianna had her back to us.

She knew what Brianna was to me and had given me plenty of lip for not seizing the chance to be with her.

The women finally left, and I rose from my pedestal. I'd only intended to watch the candidates to help Lana decide which one to hire. I simply hadn't expected Brianna to show up as one of them.

I should have known, though.

Indeed, I should have. It always struck me as too much of a coincidence that she would go into architectural engineering specializing in churches and historical monuments. What better place to find and interact with gargoyles?

The thought of her groping other gargoyle statues the way she had me stirred an irrational anger within me. I knew she hadn't encountered any other Khargals. I had warned them of her interest in us, and they would have told me had she run into any of them. Then again, seeing how the few of us still alive were scattered all over the world, the chances of her meeting any of them were slim to none.

I waited a short while before making my way up. Lana would have taken Brianna to the entrance or to her office, clearing the way for me to sneak back to my quarters upstairs. Listening to Brianna talking, I already knew we would hire her. Even without her confidence in being able to deliver on time, I was done avoiding her. The feel of her hands on my body haunted me. I needed more. I would *have* more.

Thanks to the sigils reactivating, in a few weeks, I'd be going home. Taking Brianna with me would somewhat bypass the Prime Directive. She didn't have anyone. Well, she still had her father, but last I checked, they had become estranged over the years. Would she consider leaving her home world to follow an alien being she believed to be a gargoyle?

Pacing for what felt like an eternity, I waited for Lana to finish with Brianna and come give me an update. Losing patience, I was reaching for my phone to send her a text message when the door to my private quarters finally opened. Despite the amused expression on her face, her eyes held a far more serious glint.

"She's a lovely girl," Lana said. "Still obsessed with meeting you, although she did a good job of not being too obvious this time. She also seems incredibly competent despite her youth."

"She did seem talented," I said noncommittally.

"When?" Lana asked, the mocking tone resurfacing. "When she was groping you or when she was describing the work that would need to be done before removing the rubble?"

I glared at her to hide my embarrassment and how the reminder had blood rushing to my groin again.

"Brianna wasn't groping me," I mumbled, wondering why I felt the need to lie in her defense.

"Really?" Lana said with an eyebrow raised dubiously. "I distinctly recall her hand rubbing all over your crotch."

I huffed—although it came out sounding more like a growl—and turned away from her to hide the fact that my boner was rearing its head again. Picking up my perception filter from the shelf of my living area, I pretended to fiddle with it.

"You saw wrong," I said, putting an end to that topic. "So, we're hiring her? Her firm?"

Lana nodded. "Yes. Brianna is surprisingly efficient. She already had the ball rolling, putting a whole lot of people on standby in case we gave her the contract.

She's confident the work can begin the day after tomorrow."

"Two days wasted?" I asked in protest. "I need this dug up within a week."

Lana gave me the 'stop being such a diva' look and plopped herself in my black, leather chair in a deliberate attempt to rile me up. She knew I didn't like it when people sat in *my* chair. The matching couch, and the stools by the bar, offered plenty of other seating for guests—not that I ever really received any.

"Relax. Frankly, that's record time considering she's also getting us the construction permit," Lana said. "The poor thing probably won't sleep for the next 48 hours to get everything ready in time. This is a career-making deal for her. She pulls this off for her firm, you better believe they'll make her a partner."

"For digging out rubble?" I asked, confused.

"No, silly stone head," Lana said, rolling her eyes. "For the expansion in the catacombs. It's going to be a major undertaking, with lots of bragging rights once it's done... in a few months."

"Right..."

I put the perception filter back on the shelf and flexed my wings. This would indeed be a career-defining project. Would she pick it over me?

Why in Lar's name am I thinking about that?

Okay, she had gotten my glands excited. That didn't mean she would have any interest in me. We probably had less than a month before I had to leave. That was hardly enough time for us to get to know each other enough for her to make an informed choice. For the first time, I kicked myself for not following Lana's advice, all those years ago, to seize the day.

"She will want to meet you once the work is under way to discuss your plans for the various rooms in the catacombs so that she can start working on some layouts," Lana said in a soft voice.

I walked over to the large window overlooking the small park surrounded by high-rises in the heart of downtown. Hundreds of pedestrians hurried through the streets, some of them already wearing thick sweaters or windbreakers in the sunny but cool early October morning.

"I will meet her when she returns on Thursday."

"Seriously?"

Looking over my shoulder at her, I smiled at her shocked expression. "Like you said, sometimes, one should seize the moment."

Lana sobered, rose to her feet, and approached me slowly. I turned to face her. She cupped my face in her hands with the motherly look she often gave her son. My chest tightened. Despite being centuries older than she was, Lana had become a big sister and almost a mother to me.

"She still stirs that… bonding reaction in you?" she asked softly.

I nodded.

"Then do not waste time. Whatever happens, you will never have a chance unless you try. I can't go where you are going. But wherever you end up, it would be good for me to know there's a nice lady looking after you."

"I'm not a child," I said, frowning.

"You're a man. Same thing."

Pulling my face towards hers, she stood on her tippy toes

and kissed my forehead. I snorted and shook my head. She caressed my cheek then turned and left.

The next two days dragged on forever. I reached out to the few Khargals I was still in contact with. They, too, were scrambling to recover their own sigils. Not only did we need them to find the rendezvous point but, in my case, I also had my armor, shield and weapon stashed with the sigil. While we could send a self-destruct signal to any sigil we failed to recover, that wouldn't work with my gear. I couldn't risk leaving them behind for fear humans would eventually stumble on them and reverse engineer all of my military-grade equipment. Over the past century, their technological evolution had been truly phenomenal and now grew exponentially every year. In their hands—at least in the hands of the less scrupulous ones—the sigils could be used for great evil.

I had expected Roc, a human-Khargal hybrid who also lived here in Montreal, to want to make the trip with me, but he was off to try to awaken his father from hibernation. Roc and I weren't close, being completely opposite personalities. Mischievous, the unrepentant little thief had no respect for the Prime Directive. I'd actually had to ban him from my clubs for being such a womanizer. Still, back on Duras, he wouldn't have anyone, and wouldn't know our world.

There would be time to discuss this once we were on our way home.

For now, I had an appointment with a human female who distracted me from my duty. And a warrior never strayed from his duty.

❧ 4 ❧

BRIANNA

L ana ushered me inside the club. It took all my control not to look over her shoulder in search of Alkor Drayvus. I still couldn't believe that he had agreed to meet with me, at long last. To my delight—but not Lana's—the workers had arrived at 7:00 A.M. and the reinforcement work had already begun. Stephen, the construction manager, gave me a quick update on the progress, confirming that things were not only right on track but that, barring any unforeseen complications, we would likely finish earlier than expected.

That pleased me tremendously. The sooner we were done clearing up the rubble, the sooner we'd start building the expansion. Which meant, the more time I'd get to spend with Mr. Dark and Mysterious. While surveying the work done so far, which included reinforcing all areas of the catacomb, I edged my way towards the main room and the gargoyle statue that had become a real obsession since I'd first seen it. My hands literally ached for its unusual feel, cool with an odd mix of rough yet polished stone beneath my palms. My face heated thinking of the steamy and oh so kinky dreams involving that statue and me that had kept me awake over the past two nights.

But above all, it was that gargoyle's face that haunted me. As a child, that face had been both a balm to my broken heart, and a nightmare that chased me. He had been the hero who had saved me from certain death from the icy cold water which kept rising, making my body numb, and threatening to steal my breath away. But he was also the face that appeared in the dark, murky water where my mother's lifeless body had sunk. The face that reminded me that she was never coming back home, and that Dad had never recovered from her loss. And worse still, that Dad could never forgive me for looking so much like her, like the true love he'd never see again.

And yet, two days ago, it wasn't any of those emotions that this face stirred within me. Seen through the eyes of a woman—granted, a woman with abandonment issues and strange tastes in men—his unusual beauty had mesmerized me. I'd never had a single tattoo or piercing—other than my earlobes—and I'd always thought people heavily into that stuff to be weird. But looking at that gargoyle, those facial bones and horns had been beyond sexy. The few times I'd been allowed inside The Darkest Hour during the club's operating hours, I'd been rather turned off by some of the over the top—often poorly done—implants people had gotten. But that statue…

It suddenly made me wonder if this was why Alkor always remained in the shadows. Had the plastic surgeons done a bad job of his implants? The man that had rescued me, at least in the chaotic memory I held of that day, had looked natural. For years after that, I believed gargoyles to be real. But just like kids stop believing in Santa Claus, I eventually stopped believing in flying creatures with horns who kept watch over the helpless in the night.

As I re-entered the main room, my eyes immediately flicked to the left corner where the gargoyle pedestal still sat… empty.

"Where is it?" I whispered, panic rising.

Looking frantically around—not like there was anything to look at besides stone walls and rubble—I turned to chase after Stephen to demand to know what he had done with the statue when I hit a human wall. If not for his swift reaction, catching me by the upper arms, I would have landed on my ass.

"Ow!" I said, rubbing my face.

"Sorry," a deep, gravelly voice said. "I hadn't expected you to try to tackle me out of the blue."

I couldn't tell if he were making fun of me or not. Tall, broad, and muscular, he clearly wasn't one of the construction workers. There was something familiar about his face, yet I had never met him before. Square jaw, the strangest hue of yellowish-brown eyes, and shoulder-length black hair, he was ruggedly handsome. I should have been all weak in the knees, but all I could see was the gargoyle's face.

"I… I'm sorry," I said, taking a couple of steps back. "I need to find Stephen. There was a giant gargoyle statue here and—" I said pointing at the bare pedestal.

"I moved it," the man interrupted.

I stared at him, mouth gaping. "Excuse me?"

"I moved it," the man repeated. "It wouldn't make sense to leave it here in harm's way during the construction work, don't you agree?"

My heart skipped a beat as I finally realized who was standing before me. Too stunned to respond, my gaze roamed over him, lingering on his face. Yes, the size and height matched the man I had seen from a distance, but no horns, no wings, no implants.

"You're normal," I blurted out, my voice hiding none of my disappointment.

He recoiled in surprise while my cheeks all but burst into flames.

"I mean… Oh wow, I'm so sorry. I… It's just…"

Mortified couldn't even begin to describe how I felt right now.

"What is normal? And why so disappointed?" the man I assumed to be Alkor asked. "How did you picture me, Ms. Brent? Walking around day and night looking like a creature straight out of the Underworld?"

"Well… yes?" I said with a bit of an embarrassed shrug.

"I'm sorry not to live up to your expectations then," he said, teasingly. "Should I go put on a disguise?"

"Of course not," I said, wondering if I could make things any worse. "Can we… can we start this whole mess over?" I asked. "Hi, my name is Brianna Brent, your engineer. Pleased to meet you at last."

I extended a hand, hoping he wouldn't leave me hanging.

To my relief, he smiled and took my hand. His grip, firm but gentle, baffled me. While callused popped to mind, it didn't quite fit the feel of his palms. There was a harder, grittier edge to it. Not unpleasant, but definitely strange. Still, it remained far preferable to sweaty, clammy hands. The mere thought of that gave me an icky sensation.

"Alkor Drayvus at your service," he says, his gravelly voice sounding almost like a purr. "Do you—"

The drilling sounds resumed as the workers ended their pause, interrupting Alkor. With a slightly amused smirk he gestured with his head for me to follow him. I gave him a grateful smile and shadowed him as he walked back up the stairs.

"Let's go to my office," Alkor said. "We'll be more at ease to speak."

I nodded, excited at the thought of visiting the upper floor which I'd only ever peeked at from the ground floor, or through pictures posted online by the 'cool' people with access to the VIP sections. However, instead of heading towards the small elevator at the back of the church, he opened a heavy, wooden door a few meters from the stairs to the catacombs. It opened on a room which I guessed used to serve as a small chapel for private services.

Curiosity soon pushed aside this second disappointment. The natural light through the original stained glass windows lit the room with a special aura. The eclectic furniture within came from different eras in an oddly artistic mishmash. From medieval to Victorian, modern to tribal, some of the pieces looked like they belonged in a museum. A few dark, wooden shelves displayed various objects that once again resembled original artifacts. I knew Alkor to be wealthy—at least, so stated all the rumors about him. But the value of his collection looked like it would range in multiples of millions. Why would he have such treasures so easily accessible?

"Have a seat, Ms. Brent," Alkor said, indicating a dark red couch that could have come right out of a vampire movie. "May I offer you something to drink?" he asked when I complied. "Water? Coffee? Soda? Something stronger?"

"Water would be fine," I said, although I could have used something stronger. But I needed to keep my wits about me, and my nerves couldn't handle any caffeine right now.

He pulled out a bottle of water from a mini-fridge cleverly hidden by what I had originally assumed to be a decorative wall carving.

"Oh, no need for a glass," I said when he reached for one on his minibar. "I'm not a very formal kind of girl."

His pleased smile told me I'd earned some brownie points. Why that mattered, who knew? But for some reason, it did.

"I want to thank you for giving me this opportunity to do the work for you, Mr. Drayvus," I said, remembering the 'always butter up the important client' rule my firm insisted upon.

"Alkor, please," he said, taking a seat in the matching chair across from me. "You'll find that I, too, am not particularly formal."

I believed it, and yet, there was something solemn about him. He used common words when he spoke and, still, he managed to come off as… not necessarily stuck up, but definitely of another level of society. I couldn't tell if it was the way he subtly dragged certain syllables, that gravelly voice of his, or how he pronounced words as if they had different flavors he savored. Princely came to mind…

"Certainly. But then I must insist you call me Brianna."

He gave me the bottle, which I accepted graciously, and then resumed his seat.

"Brianna it is," he said, resting his ankle on his knee, his smile stretching. "And you only got the contract based on your own merit. You came prepared, with a clear plan, your team ready to go. You met my needs where others failed. I should be the one thanking you for delivering on such short notice. I am pleased with the progress so far."

I preened under his approval. This contract could make my career. Talk about killing two birds with one stone. Although I'd met my mystery man, I still needed answers. But how could I bring it up without tipping my hand?

"I'm very happy as well," I said, hiding none of the pride I felt. "Stephen is my go-to person whenever I need work done fast and well. We've collaborated on many contracts, and he's always delivered on my plans. I'm sure you will be very satisfied with the results." I shifted on my seat and nervously licked my lip. "This is why I almost panicked when I saw the gargoyle statue missing. Like everything you possess," I said waving at all the artifacts in his office, "it seemed of tremendous value. If something had happened to it..."

"It is invaluable to me," Alkor said with a nod when my voice trailed off. "Therefore, leaving it in the middle of a construction site seemed ill-advised."

"Right," I said, tucking a strand of my golden-brown hair behind my ear. "I have to admit that I'm fascinated by it. It is in such great condition, I'm assuming it's been recently made. Do you know the model?"

Alkor tilted his head to the side and gave me an unreadable look. "Why do you ask?"

I fiddled with my bottle of water, screwing and

unscrewing the lid in an obvious tell of how nervous I felt. "He… he reminds me of someone special. Someone who played a major role in my life."

Alkor raised an inquisitive eyebrow. "Oh?"

"He…" I stopped and took a sip of water, my throat suddenly feeling utterly dry. My gut told me Alkor knew exactly who the model was. "He saved my life many years ago. I never had a chance to thank that man. If it's him…"

"A man with horns and facial bones saved your life?" Alkor asked.

My face heated, knowing what kind of thoughts had to be crossing his mind right now. "His features are the same," I said, dodging the actual question. "The eyes, the nose, the mouth, the square jaw, and that wavy, fluffy hair. You are well-known for your amazing disguise as well. And yet, right now, you couldn't be more…"

"Normal?" he said, teasingly when my voice trailed off.

My cheeks burned again.

"Would you like to see me with horns and wings, Brianna?"

"Yes!" I blurted out way too quickly.

Alkor burst out laughing. "Well, someone is certainly eager."

"I'm sorry. Wow," I said, mortified. "I'm usually more controlled and—"

"Do not fret," Alkor said. "Your spontaneity is refreshing. Come back tomorrow night, when the club opens. You'll be allowed up the elevator to my box to see, first-hand, the Lord of The Darkest Hour."

"Really?" I asked, leaning forward in my excitement. "I

mean, you don't have to. I don't want to make you feel like…
You know. I…"

"Yes, really," Alkor said, his eyes sparkling with amusement. "And no, you won't make me feel like a freak show any more than I normally do. I wouldn't have offered otherwise."

I hesitated, not quite knowing how to answer that.

"All right, then," I said lamely. "Thank you. I would like that very much."

"Don't forget the dress code," he added.

My stomach dropped as I mentally reviewed my wardrobe. I didn't have anything hardcore gothic. But I did have a bohemian blouse with puffy sleeves, and a long black skirt. I could buy myself a gothic necklace and dark lipstick on the way home today. This was too great an opportunity to miss. I'd make it work.

"I won't," I said, feeling giddy.

It struck me then that Alkor had deftly shifted the topic away from the man who had modeled for the gargoyle. Taking a sip of water, I contemplated bringing back the topic but couldn't think of a way to do so that wouldn't make me stalkerish or creepy. There would be other opportunities.

Forcing myself to focus on the reason for my presence here, I turned my attention back to my mandate. "Now, about the contract, I would need more details about what you want to do with those rooms so that I can start drawing some first drafts for your approval. I was also wondering what type of event you are planning in that first room. It is fairly small. There's still time to open up one of the other, more spacious rooms instead while respecting your deadline."

"No," Alkor said sharply. The finality of his tone took me aback. "I need this specific room done. No other."

"Okay," I said in a careful tone. "It was just a suggestion."

"And a thoughtful one. Thank you," Alkor replied in a conciliatory voice. "But it needs to be this room. It is... special."

"All right," I said. Sensing that he wouldn't welcome me prying further, I dropped the topic.

Alkor then proceeded to tell me his plans for the twelve rooms in the catacombs. Thankfully, the mortal remains had been moved before he bought the church, so we wouldn't have to deal with that. The project sounded ambitious—definitely a career defining undertaking for someone like me. Each room would be set up to allow themed private parties, from vampires to shifters, to necromancers and demons. But they would also be used as escape rooms, so various nooks and crannies to hide clues would be required. And last, but not least, he also wanted a few hidden passages that allowed access between rooms.

I would need to work with Elisa, one of the best interior decorators I'd ever met. Between the two of us, and the basically unlimited budget he was allowing, we would knock Alkor's socks off. By the time I finished taking down notes, my fingers felt sore, but my imagination overflowed with ideas.

As Alkor escorted me back to the entrance, I stole a few furtive glances at him. Having overcome my initial disappointment, I had to admit his charm was steadily growing on me, not to mention he had a body to die for. Tomorrow night would prove quite interesting.

"Goodbye, Brianna," Alkor said, with that crazy, sexy voice of his. "I look forward to seeing you again tomorrow evening."

"Believe me, no more than I do," I said, that wretched eagerness rearing its annoying head again.

Alkor snorted, a strange glimmer flicking through his uncanny yellow eyes. "Indeed," he said, a mysterious smile stretching his full lips.

"Until tomorrow, then," I said before leaving.

As I walked out in the cool late morning breeze, Alkor's stare burned holes in my back. But I kept my head straight, refusing to look back and reveal how much our meeting had affected me. Tomorrow couldn't come soon enough.

I ended up shopping after all and found this ridiculously sexy, black brocade, steampunk corset with golden clasps in the front, making it so much easier to close. A black flannel, ruffled long-sleeve bolero coat gave the outfit a bit more flair, which I completed with a short, black leather skirt and a pair of high-heeled, steampunk, black ankle boots. I let my golden-brown hair down, the natural waves nicely framing my face, and kept the makeup to a minimum— mainly some mascara and a nude lipstick.

Looking at myself in the mirror, I had to admit the result was flattering. It had more of a gothic edge than steampunk vibe, which pleased me. I had this vampire mistress thing going on, which I found super-hot. Considering we were still a little over three weeks away from Halloween, I covered my outfit with a long, black leather coat, not wanting my nosy neighbors to start asking questions if they ran into me on my way to the garage.

After dropping my car in a nearby underground parking

garage, I walked nervously up to the entrance of The Darkest Hour. A line had already formed outside with eager patrons in a variety of impressive outfits. The doorman recognized me, but his eyes narrowed at my 'traditional' coat. I shrugged it off, revealing my more suitable clothing beneath. With an approving smile, he gestured me in, ahead of the pack. I'd never been part of the 'in-crowd' that got to skip ahead of the line before. It felt freaking awesome! I loved their envious stares, each wondering who I was, and what made me so special.

I've got a date with the big boss, bitches! Eat your hearts out!

The party was already in full swing inside. Throngs of people had taken the dance floor by storm, others sipped exotic looking drinks served in skull-shaped glasses, or with smoke at the top as if dry-ice had been dropped into their beverages. Most booths along the walls were already full, laden with bottles and munchies for the wealthy patrons occupying them. But I had no time for any of this. My heart pulsed in tandem with the pounding beat of the music playing as I made my way to the back, towards the private elevator. Another security guard, whose name I didn't remember, nodded at me as I approached. He opened the cage door of the elevator and gestured with his head for me to go in. He used a key fob on the security panel and then pressed the up button before stepping outside and closing the door behind him.

The lift flew up, and my shoulders tensed with anxiety, anticipation, and the terrifying sense that something important was about to happen; a line would be crossed, and there would be no turning back from this.

The lift stopped on the private balcony which only Alkor

had access to. With a trembling hand, I opened the cage door and stepped out. Alkor, his back turned to me, was looking down at the partying crowd, his hands resting on the railing. Two massive, leather wings with vicious looking spurs at the top and at the tips, hung folded on his back. They flexed, the motion incredibly natural for mechanized prosthetics.

"Welcome, Brianna," Alkor said, without turning around. His voice sounded deeper and even more gravelly than before.

"Hi," I whispered, struggling to find my voice.

He turned his face sideways, giving me a profile view. My stomach dropped at the sight of the facial bones and short horns protruding from his hair.

I knew that face. But the darkness kept me from being certain. I advanced with hesitant steps, my breath coming in short bursts as if too much pressure on my chest kept me from breathing properly. Stopping barely two feet behind him, his long tail twitched as I raised my hand, fingers trembling, and reached for his right wing. Still looking at me over his shoulder, Alkor stretched that wing, allowing me to explore its soft, leathery texture. A network of veins crisscrossed the dark membrane between the bones. My palm roamed over it, then towards the middle of his back, where it attached seamlessly on the side of his spine beneath his shoulder blade. No contraption strapped it to his body.

"They are real," I whispered. "You are real."

Alkor turned around, his face devoid of any expression, although a muscle ticked at the edge of his jaw. My chin quivered, and my eyes misted as I looked upon the face that had haunted my dreams for the past twenty years. The strong jaw, the yellow eyes, the prominent forehead, and sensual lips. With a will of their own, my hands cupped his face, tracing every single one of his features as if to confirm what I was seeing. Alkor closed his eyes, and his lips parted as he surrendered himself to my touch. A sharp pair of fangs peeked out from between them. The blunted tips of his horns scraped my palms, while the silky feel of his dark-brown hair soothed them.

"It's you. It's you," I repeated in a litany, tears I couldn't control trickling down my cheeks. "I found you. After all these years, I found you."

Throwing my arms around his neck, I buried my face in his chest and bawled my eyes out. His arm wrapping around my back and his hand caressing my hair only opened the floodgates wider. In that instant, it wasn't just emotional gratitude overwhelming me, but the fear, the sorrow, and the loss I had sustained that day, and in the years that followed, that all came crashing back down on me.

"Hush, Brianna. Hush," Alkor whispered, still gently stroking my hair. "I am here. You are safe. It's over. No harm can come to you anymore."

I tightened my hold around him and nodded, deeply moved that he had understood without requiring an explanation. My face rubbed against his neck, the texture of his skin slightly rough, like his hand had been yesterday when I shook it. Forcing myself to get a grip, I reluctantly loosened my hold and looked up at him, feeling rather embarrassed. His yellow eyes gazed upon me with such tenderness that my chest constricted. He gently wiped my tears with his knuckles and placed a kiss on my forehead.

"Why?" I asked softly. "Why did you hide from me all these years? Why reveal yourself now?"

A troubled expression crossed his unusual features, and he averted his eyes.

"Please," I begged. "I need to know. You knew who I was all these years when you refused to see me, didn't you?"

Alkor sighed then nodded. "I was trying to protect both of us. Come," he said. His hand on my waist, he led me to a large, cushioned, leather bench.

Despite the dim lights, I could see that the sparse furniture in the large private booth was top quality. Once again, most of the pieces appeared to be antiques. Aside from the bench, a matching chair and three-cushion couch surrounding a wooden coffee table, the booth possessed its own minibar, a circular table that could seat ten people, and a set of five monitors that displayed all key areas of the club in rotation.

I sat on the bench, and Alkor settled next to me, our arms touching.

"Protect me by hiding that you're a gargoyle?" I asked gently. "That statue was you, right?"

Alkor smiled. "That statue was indeed me, but I'm not a gargoyle. I'm a Khargal."

I blinked, unsure of the difference. "Is that a different breed of gargoyles?"

Alkor chuckled. "The gargoyle is a human myth inspired by Khargals. My kind has been among humans for centuries, living in hiding. But the occasional sighting is inevitable. Humans created their own lore based on real events, but also based on a great deal of assumption and speculation."

"Okay, but where do you come from? Where do your people normally live?" I asked. "I mean, you're not really from some kind of Underworld, right?"

Alkor burst out laughing. "No, Brianna. I do not come

from the Underworld. Truth be told, there are very few of my kind around. In fact, just a little over twenty."

"Twenty?" I exclaimed, my eyes widening. "What happened? You were hunted? You don't have many children?"

"Our females here all died," Alkor said in a somber tone. "A few of my brothers have taken human mates with whom they've had hybrid offspring."

"Oh, I'm so sorry. It was inconsiderate of me to pry like this," I said, mortified by my lack of tact.

"It's okay," Alkor said, with a gentle smile. "It happened a long time ago. But as you can guess, the less people know about us, the better. Certain unsavory groups would love to get their hands on us to turn us into lab rats."

The way he said that, he'd clearly already dealt with some of said 'unpleasant' individuals.

"So why did you finally agree to reveal yourself to me now?"

"Some things have… changed. Things that make me reconsider my stance about certain… situations."

"Some things like whatever it is that makes you want to reopen that room?" I asked.

Alkor narrowed his eyes at me, and I held his gaze, daring him to contradict me.

"Yes," he conceded. "Some things like that."

"What are you really after? What's your agenda?" I asked. "What do you want?"

"There are many things I want, Brianna. *Many* things." Alkor said, his eyes dipping to my mouth. "But that is for another time."

I licked my lips in an involuntary, nervous gesture. His

yellow eyes darkened, turning to molten gold. My stomach fluttered as his gaze remained glued to my mouth.

"You can trust me, you know?" I said, leaning forward. "You saved my life. My father's life as well. I would never betray you or harm you."

"I want to trust you," he whispered. "I want…"

His voice trailed off, replaced by an almost animalistic growl. And then his lips were pressing against mine. I couldn't say for sure who had kissed whom as I'd been fighting the urge to throw myself at him. I welcomed his invading tongue, a fiery ball of desire swirling in my belly. My fingers found their way through his hair, the horns making it a little awkward to fiddle through them. In a move so swift it made my head spin, Alkor effortlessly lifted me with one hand under my bum and positioned me to straddle his lap. His mouth swallowed my yelp of surprise as he dove in for seconds.

Although not prudish, I didn't make a habit of jumping a man I felt attracted to. But this man… this Khargal… I wanted him to ravage me. And Alkor seemed just as hungry for me. Tilting my head back, he covered my neck with kisses, his fangs scraping over my sensitive skin making my stomach quiver with fear and excitement. His hand lowered to my bum, pressing me against his pelvis. The stiffness rubbing against my core left no mystery as to his level of arousal.

Only when I felt my bustier loosen did I realize that Alkor had opened the first two clasps. Bending me farther back, he continued to unclasp the others while the warm wetness of his mouth closed around my nipple. I threw my head back and moaned, pleasure coursing through me from both my breast and the wickedly divine friction of his groin against mine. My short skirt having ridden up meant my thong in no way dulled the sensation of his hard cock rubbing against me. Alkor, bare-chested, wore only a skin-tight, grey pair of pants, of an unknown fabric, that also allowed me to feel him as if he were fully naked.

My bustier fell off and Alkor drew me back to him, recapturing my lips. The burning skin of his bare chest against mine tore another moan from me. His arms around my back held me with incredible possessiveness, like he feared I would flee or disappear. No thought could be further from my mind.

"I want you," Alkor growled against my lips, the urgency in his voice making my stomach flip-flop and my inner walls throb. "I need you."

"Yes," I whispered, my voice trembling with an irrational desire.

Alkor growled again, his hand slipping around and under my bum, his fingers parting the thin fabric of my thong to tease the seam of my pussy. A strangled moan escaped me, and I writhed under his ministrations, needing more.

"You're already wet... So *gracking* wet for me," Alkor said.

"I need you," I said, echoing his earlier words, aching to feel him inside me.

I felt—more than I saw—him free his cock. And then its head was pushing against my opening. Despite the slickness of my arousal, it proved a tight fit. Alkor worked his way in with a series of shallow thrusts. It took every ounce of my willpower not to just impale myself on his shaft, the need to feel him deep inside me overriding every other thought, and even, almost, my sense of self-preservation.

"You're mine," Alkor said, his voice thick with desire, once fully sheathed. "You're all mine now."

His wings wrapped around us as he began to pump in and out of me. Each stroke awakened me to a whole new world of sensations. I hadn't seen his cock, but I could feel the unusual ridges along its length caressing me just the right way inside.

Alkor's labored breath in my ear, and his sultry moans further fanned the fire consuming me from within. The odd texture of his skin tickled every single one of my nerve endings. He was inside me, all around me, taking me to sinfully delicious heights as I began to crest. Heart pounding, skin burning, I toppled over the edge as the raging inferno in the depths of my core erupted in blissful waves of ecstasy. My body seized, and I cried out his name. Alkor continued to pump furiously in and out of me, his bruising hold tightening around me as he neared his own climax.

"Brianna," Alkor said. "Brianna!" he repeated, this time as if in pain.

Through blurred vision, still coming down from my own high, I watched him swallow painfully, his fangs bared, a hungry look on his face as if he were struggling not to bury them in my neck. And then, he threw his head back, shouting his release, his wings spreading wide open behind him. His seed shot deep inside me and, for a fleeting moment, I realized we hadn't used protection. And yet, for some reason, I couldn't bring myself to worry. Body still shaking with the tremors of his orgasm, Alkor looked at me with such wonder and borderline worship, I melted against him.

Still buried deep, he once again closed his wings around us and kissed me slowly, tenderly.

"My woman," Alkor whispered against my lips. "I'm keeping you."

I didn't know what to say to that, but he didn't seem to expect a reply. For the next eternity, our hearts beating in tandem with the rhythmic thumping of the music inside the club, we remained in each other's embrace, savoring this moment of intimacy in the aftermath.

ALKOR

I couldn't stop feasting my eyes on my woman as she peacefully slept in my bed. Despite taking her four times already—three yesterday evening and waking her for another round during the night—I hungered for her still. My mating glands had swelled at the back of my throat, demanding to release my *dassa*, for the mating kiss. The binding fluid would make her my life mate. Same with my fangs, which ached to complete the bonding bite. Although not required, it would accelerate the process. But I couldn't do this lightly, and especially not without her consent. The consequences were too great. The lack of sex in my life didn't explain this insatiable need she'd awakened in me. Khargals weren't slaves to their libido. Unless we found our mate, our sexual drive remained fairly minimal.

But mate or not, by revealing myself to Brianna, and worse still, by becoming intimate with her, I'd stomped all over the Prime Directive. As a career soldier, and high-ranking officer, I'd always taken pride in following rules and enforcing laws—not breaking them. For a millennium, I had resisted temptation, even over the past twenty years since meeting Brianna—although the last ten, once she came of age, had proven to be the truly painful ones.

The few women I had been intimate with over that thousand years, only once each, had no idea of my true nature. I'd also made sure not to impregnate them. Reproducing with humans would be an even bigger violation of the rules. A few of my brothers had done so. I had severely frowned upon their actions, but stranded and alone for centuries, it felt heartless to begrudge them finding what bit of happiness they could.

Back then, I hadn't believed a human female could stir our mating instincts. But meeting Brianna had flipped that notion on its head. Still, I had remained steadfast in my observance of the rules, agonizing each day at the thought my woman was aging and soon, her short human lifespan would permanently take her from me. That she'd still been in her twenties had made it an easier choice. But would my resolve have remained unshakable as she grew older?

Last night, I had broken all of those rules and ached to break them further. Biting Brianna, sharing my mating fluids with her, would increase her lifespan and make her body stronger, less vulnerable to sickness, cold, heat, and deprivations of all types. It would also prepare her to receive my child and allow a successful implantation.

Brianna stirred. Her eyelids fluttered, and she stretched her long, toned limbs. The blanket slipped, exposing mouthwatering pink nipples. Unable to resist their appeal, I wrapped my lips around her left one. Startled, Brianna emitted a shocked cry, which turned into an amused chuckle. Her fingers weaved through my hair while I sucked on her hardening little nub.

I loved the sweet taste of her and the softness of her skin. Shoving the blanket aside, revealing her sexy nakedness, I let my hands roam over her flat stomach before dipping between her legs. Her breath caught, and her back arched. Brianna's response to my touch drove me crazy. Already, the proof of her arousal coated my fingers. I pursued my manual assault until she fell apart, and only then did I bury myself into the searing warmth of her tight sheath. The wet embrace of her inner walls around my cock set my blood ablaze, each stroke sending electric sparks up my spine and to all of my nerve endings.

My mating glands swelled further. The primal need to bind her tortured me beyond words. Her delicate hands, feverishly exploring me, impatient and possessive, helped distract me from this torment. They awakened sensations unlike anything I'd ever imagined. Brianna had already become an addiction I couldn't—wouldn't—let go of. I pounded into her with reckless abandon, forcing myself to rub my pelvis against hers, every five thrusts or so to stimulate her clitoris just the right way.

When a violent climax swept her away, her inner walls clamping down on me forced my own orgasm from me. Holding her tight, I buried my cock deep as my seed shot forth in a blissful flow. We kissed—a practice uncommon for my people but one I greatly enjoyed—and remained in each other's embrace until our hearts and breaths settled down.

With much reluctance, I finally pulled out of Brianna and led her by the hand to the bathroom. While we showered together, she took a good look at my privates for the first time. The ridges along its length fascinated her.

"So that's what had been torturing me in the most wonderful way," she whispered, crouching in front of me to get a better look.

My abdominal muscles contracted and my shaft jerked in response to her fingers carefully rubbing over my ridges. Seconds later, her mouth closed around my cock. Brianna worked me with her divine lips and tongue, stroking me in counterpoint to her mouth's movements until I climaxed again. Her surprised moan of pleasure reached me through the lustful haze in which I drowned.

I blinked, looking down at her as she first licked her lips and then the lingering drops of semen on my shaft.

"Dude… You taste like salted caramel! You are so getting blow jobs often!"

I gaped at her as she rose to her feet before bursting out laughing. "Well, that's one promise I certainly will not complain about," I said drawing her into my arms.

The shrill sound of the alarm on her phone startled us out of the tender kiss we'd begun exchanging.

"Fuck! I'm going to be late for work," Brianna exclaimed. She hurried through the rest of her shower and then rushed through drying herself. "Please tell me you have some kind of shirt I can borrow," she said. "I can't go to work wearing that bustier. The skirt and shoes will raise eyebrows, but I can get away with them."

I didn't really have shirts. They didn't play well with wings and would look odd once I went into stone form. My perception filter spared me the trouble, anyway.

"Hmm, would your employer frown at a t-shirt from The Darkest Hour?" I asked.

Brianna chewed her bottom lip for a second. "No. It should be fine. It's classy, and black always looks nice. The only problem is I have no bra and the damn boardrooms are always chilly."

"You have the most perfect breasts," I said, tweaking one of her nipples. Round and perky, the perfect size to fit in my hands, her breasts were begging for my attention again.

"Hey!" she exclaimed, swatting at my hand.

I chuckled and reached for my perception filter wrist bracer. Brianna's stare weighed heavily on me as I put it on. Before I could activate it, her palm rubbed over my wingless back, her fingers lingering on the barely visible slit beneath my shoulder blade. She examined it with an expression of wonder.

"I still can't get over the fact that you can make your wings disappear and then grow them back," she whispered.

The flabbergasted look on Brianna's face when I'd tucked away my wings last night after I first brought her to my bed still made me chuckle.

"I don't exactly 'grow' them back, but yes, it is most practical to be able to tuck them away. They make sleeping in a bed quite uncomfortable. That tail though," I said, casting a disgruntled glance at it, "there's no getting rid of it."

Brianna laughed as I tucked my tail in my pants and made it wrap around my right leg.

"I'll be right back with the t-shirt," I said, activating my perception filter.

Her eyes widened as I took on the appearance of the average-looking man she had first met in the catacombs, wearing a black shirt and leather pants. As I raced down the stairs, rather than using the lift, I pondered again the wisdom of revealing so much to Brianna, so quickly—of stomping so recklessly all over the Prime Directive.

She's mine. She's my mate.

Indeed, she was. Yesterday evening, throughout the night, and this morning again, she had willingly given herself to me. Even now, the taste of her lingered on my tongue. I hadn't revealed the most important parts, yet. She needed to be eased into the whole truth. For the first time, I felt grateful for rescuing her all those years ago. That encounter had mentally prepared her to accept my existence.

I raced back upstairs to find her drying her hair. She slipped on the t-shirt. As she feared, her nipples broadcast the absence of a bra, making me want to tear it right off and toss her back on my bed. I resisted the urge. This wasn't how I had intended to start off our relationship. No matter how insatiable she made me feel, Brianna needed to know my interest in her wasn't purely sexual.

"Will you have dinner with me tonight," I asked, watching her quickly brush her hair.

"I would love… Oh," she said, her face passing from excited to deflated. "I already had plans for tonight. Maybe you could come with me?" Brianna said, hope shining in her eyes.

"Maybe," I said cautiously. "What kind of plans?"

"I have a ticket for the Gardens of Light at the Botanical Garden. My firm gave it to me in preparation for an upcoming project. They had offered me two tickets but since I didn't have a date to bring along, I passed. But if you'd like to come with… You know, I… I would really enjoy your company."

She'd spoken quickly, the slight trembling in her voice and the widening of her eyes, betraying her nervousness and obvious fear of being rejected.

Silly female.

I'd been racking my brains trying to come up with some nice activity to do with her as human males did during courtship. She'd just made things easier for me.

"I would be delighted to accompany you," I said, a strange warmth spreading through my chest as she beamed at me. "But I do not mind buying my own ticket."

Brianna shook her head. "They will be sold out for tonight. And the firm won't mind." She picked up her coat and smiled gratefully when I helped her put it on. "I really must go. I have a stupid pitch to make to the big wigs. They won't be pleased if I'm late."

"It will be quite the presentation then," I said teasingly, glancing at her nipples poking through her t-shirt.

"I'll grab a bra at La Senza on my way to the office. There's one nearby."

"If it's open."

She glared at me and gave me a playful tap on the shoulder.

"Stop being such a prophet of doom!"

I chuckled and drew her into my arms. "I had a wonderful time with you, Brianna, and can't wait to get to know you better. I… I hope the feeling is mutual."

She smiled, a pretty blush rising on her cheeks. "I like you a lot, Alkor. I'm looking forward to spending more time with you."

"Good," I whispered before kissing her again.

Brianna leaned in to me and our tongues mingled for a moment before she pulled away.

"I have to go," she said softly. "I'll see you later, okay?"

I nodded and accompanied her downstairs and through the side exit of the club. A strange sense of loss washed over me as I watched her walking briskly away. With a heavy sigh, I returned to my office and called my notary.

The time had come to put my house in order.

❧ 6 ❧

BRIANNA

As Alkor had predicted, the lingerie store had been closed. Of course it would have been. Nothing opened before 10:00 AM. The clerk inside, already there to prepare the store's opening, had refused to cut me some slack. The boardroom, freezing as always, had my nipples standing at attention for the duration of the meeting. I wanted to believe the brilliance of my pitch had earned me such undivided attention from the attendees, but I knew better.

Nevertheless, the partners appeared pleased, not only with that presentation, but with the feedback they'd received so far from Lana Dalghren regarding progress at The Darkest Hour. Would they still be pleased if they knew the owner had spent the evening, night, and morning fucking my brains out? What would they say if I told them that I hadn't drunk my usual morning mochaccino because I didn't want it to spoil the lingering taste of salty caramel on my tongue from the most amazing blow job I'd ever given? How shocked would they

53

be if they found out I'd been nipple-flashing them all day as a consequence of my walk of shame?

My face heated every time I thought of the wanton way in which I'd behaved. How could I have jumped into bed barely ten minutes into our first date? Heck, it hadn't even officially been a date. After the first round on the bench of his private booth, I'd been horrified to realize people in the VIP booths could have seen us. Although Alkor reassured me that they couldn't because we'd been too far back, I couldn't help wondering if him closing his wings around us while he fucked me had been to shelter us from view.

In spite of all that, I didn't regret spending the night with Alkor. Mind-blowing didn't even begin to describe what he'd made me feel. But more than the sex itself, it was the tenderness with which he'd held, touched, and cuddled with me that had truly won me. I had worried he might have thought me an easy girl and kicked me to the curb after getting what he wanted, but nothing in his behavior indicated that he considered me a booty call. That would have crushed me.

For years, I'd dreamt of meeting my savior. Never would I have imagined it would go down this way. Although, growing up, I'd begun fantasizing about him with some pretty vivid wet dreams.

As I walked back to my car to head home, a million questions raced through my mind. In my lust craze, I hadn't asked him any of the things I'd wanted to for years. Why had he agreed to see me and reveal himself to me now? His answer had been evasive at best. Something important lay buried inside that room. Something which I feared could jeopardize whatever might be blossoming between us. But I also wanted to know more about him and his people. Where did they come from? Why were there so few of them left? And why were they living scattered, isolated from each other? Did Lana know of his true nature?

On the way home, I made a detour by the medical clinic to get myself a morning after pill, then by the pharmacy to buy a couple of boxes of condoms. If this relationship would build into something more serious—which I hoped it would—I'd need to get back on the pill. It had been irresponsible of me to think it okay to let whatever happened happen last night. A nagging voice at the back of my head insisted that it was okay to just go with the flow, but I needed to be adult about this.

As soon as I reached home, I made a beeline for my wardrobe. Before Alkor agreed to come with me, I had planned on wearing some leggings with an oversized sweater. But now, I needed something a bit more flattering, especially since I didn't know how the evening would end—although I had certain hopes.

I ended up going with a black, high-waisted, flared skirt, and a sleeveless, black leather top that zipped in front—no bra. Having learned my lesson, though, I shoved a suitable change of clothes—bra included—in a small bag which I would leave in my car, just in case. I threw a frozen pizza in the oven, kicking myself for not accepting an early dinner with Alkor. After a quick shower, I got dressed and primped up, trying not to overdo it.

As I prepared to leave, my phone rang. My heart sank at my father's distinctive ringtone.

"Hello, Dad," I answered, trying to sound friendly.

"Hey Brie," my father's voice said over the phone with his usual fake enthusiasm. "How is my girl doing?"

I barely managed not to sigh out loud as I rolled my eyes.

Like he actually cared. "I'm doing great, thanks. The partners just gave me a really big project—the kind of church project I've been dreaming of for years."

"Good, good. That's really nice, sweetie," Dad said.

Meaning: he didn't give a shit. It shouldn't upset me anymore, but his indifference still hurt.

"Any Romeo on the horizon?" he asked—just as lame a change from his usual 'any beau in sight?'

"Actually, I have met someone," I said, suddenly feeling nervous. "It's only been a few days so it's too early to tell where that will go. But I like him a lot."

"Oh! Good. Very good. A pretty girl like you shouldn't be alone."

I waited for him to ask a few questions about Alkor, even if only his name. *Nada.* Why did I keep hoping?

"So, how's Merryl?" I asked when the silence stretched uncomfortably.

"Oh, she's wonderful!" Dad exclaimed, his enthusiasm shooting into overdrive. That, too, hurt. "She's already packed half the house into her suitcases. I keep reminding her we're only going on a two-week cruise. She doesn't need all that stuff, but she's such a worry wart," he said affectionately. "She needs to be prepared for every eventuality."

"I bet," I said politely, not really wanting to hear about step-mommy dearest.

"Our trip ends in St. Martin's," Dad said, sounding excited. He cleared his throat, and I immediately knew the real reason for his call would now follow. "We're going to stay at Merryl's friend's place for the next six months. It's actually a shared vacation home. We're hoping to have our new home built by then. The contractor and his crew are ready to roll as soon as you send in the final version of the plan. So… I was wondering how that was coming along."

I bit my tongue not to respond with some snarky remark and blinked back the tears that pricked my eyes. As always, my father only ever contacted me when he wanted something or if some legal paperwork required it. He didn't call me for Christmas or Thanksgiving. As the daughter, it was *my* duty to reach out to him. Once, I'd actually played chicken with him to see who would hold out the longest without calling the other. After a year-and-a-half, I conceded victory to him.

"It's done," I said, proud that my voice didn't betray my raw emotions. "I finished it last night. I'll be sending it first thing in the morning."

That was a lie. I'd finished it last weekend and actually thought I'd already sent it. But I guess my subconscious had held on to it to force him to call me.

"Wonderful! I knew I could count on my baby girl to come through for me!" Dad exclaimed. "I'll tell Merryl the good news. She'll be ecstatic. Listen, when construction is completed, you'll have to ask your boss for a few days off to come spend time with us. As you know, there will be a guest room with your name on it."

"That's great, Dad. I'm looking forward to it."

Maybe I should try my hand at acting. I was putting on an Oscar-worthy performance.

"All right, then. I'm going to inform the contractor so that he can get ready and maybe even start the work tomorrow," Dad said, clearly eager to be on his way.

A malicious part of me thought of coming up with random topics to keep him on the phone longer, out of pure spite. But that would accomplish nothing other than make us both miserable. Plus, I had a sexy date with a garg… Khargal.

"Okay, Dad. Have a nice trip. Give my regards to Merryl."

"I will, sweetie. Take care!"

He hung up before I could say another word. The distance had steadily increased over the years, but at least he'd still been in Montreal. We didn't see each other often, but the possibility for it had existed. Now, with him and his new wife making the permanent move to St. Martin's, we would never see each other again. Father didn't care much for technology. He'd find an excuse not to get on those countless free video chats to catch up with his only child. I could fall off the face of the Earth tomorrow, he wouldn't know—or care. Well, unless he suddenly needed my engineer or architect services, or my contacts for some construction work.

Maybe Alkor will sweep me away into the Underworld or whatever the lair of the Khargals is!

Shaking off the gloomy feeling that speaking to—or even thinking about—my dad always put me in, I grabbed my purse and left the house, en route to meet with Mister horny, winged, and mysterious.

⚜

We walked hand in hand, traipsing along the path of the Montreal Botanical Garden. As expected on opening night, people had come out in droves. Thankfully, everyone acted in a civilized manner, no shoving or pushing, showing consideration when someone wanted to take pictures, or allowing them to go first.

The various displays took my breath away. In each scene,

lanterns in the shapes of animals or people presented enchanting, illuminated tableaus. I couldn't pick a favorite between the Chinese dragon, the panda family, or the fishermen by the pond. I took a million pictures, but hated that I couldn't take some of Alkor. Although he didn't fear it would penetrate his technology, he wanted to limit how many images of him—or his disguises—circulated. That didn't stop him from taking loads of pictures of me.

As we reached one of the pagodas, the crowd seemed to thin. For a moment, I wondered if we were missing some kind of exciting event that everyone else had gravitated towards. But then, having Alkor all to myself, in the dead of night, only surrounded by the colorful lights of the lanterns didn't strike me as too bad of a deal.

He looked around us, a strange expression on his face.

"What?" I asked. "Who are you looking for?"

"No one," he said. "I'm making sure no one sees us."

His air of mischief had me both tingling with excitement and tensing with worry. Grabbing my hand, he lured me into the shadows beneath a cluster of trees behind the pagoda. Pressing his chest to my back, he held me tight.

"Do not move, and do not be afraid," Alkor whispered in my ear.

That scared me.

The air shimmered before my eyes. Worried, I looked at Alkor over my shoulder in time to see his wings spread wide behind him.

"What are you doing?" I squeaked in a hushed voice.

"Giving you a better view."

And just like that, he flapped his wings, and we lifted off. Although he held me tightly, I clung to his arms, wishing I were facing him instead so that I could wrap my arms around his neck. Panicked, forcing myself not to scream, I closed my eyes, only to reopen them seconds later; the darkness freaked me out even more. Thankfully, it was a very short flight to the roof of the pagoda.

"People are going to see us!" I exclaimed in a whispered voice.

"No, they won't. I have my stealth module active," Alkor said, sounding smug. "But keep your movements to a strict minimum. It's normally only meant for one person."

"So, you mean, I could be standing buck naked up here and people would only see empty air?" I asked, looking at him over my shoulder.

"No. If you were naked right now, we'd be giving everyone an eyeful. I wouldn't be able to resist your charms, and the camouflage wouldn't be able to sustain that kind of intensity," Alkor said, his voice dipping almost an octave lower.

He stared at me, his eyes darkening, and desire spreading across his features. My nipples hardened at the thought of all the things he could be doing to me, right here on this roof. It felt odd finding myself in his embrace and becoming aroused, while his human disguise eyed me with such blatant lust. Even knowing my lover lurked beneath that mask, the thought of kissing him when he looked like someone else, would take a bit of getting used to.

"Well then, it's a good thing I'm fully dressed," I whispered.

Alkor grunted his agreement, then looked down at a loud group of people approaching the pagoda along the left side of the path. My gaze flicked to them before roaming over the garden. The view was amazing from up here. I almost felt like a Greek goddess on Mount Olympus, looking down at clusters of human cities and the unaware mortals who dwelled within.

"Are you cold?" Alkor asked.

I shook my head. "No. It's a little cool, but not unpleasantly so. Any chance we could do a flyover?" I asked, already suspecting what his answer would be.

"That would be ill-advised," Alkor said in an apologetic tone. "The risk is too great, especially with so many people around. But we can drive out of town to a more rural area, and I'll take you on a flight if you wish."

"I would love that!" I said, silencing the inner voice reminding me of my fear of heights.

His arms tightened around me, and he nuzzled my nape before giving it a gentle nip. A shiver of pleasure ran down my spine. The prickly feeling of his fang scraping over my skin had me hot and bothered in seconds.

"Then we will go this weekend, if you wish," Alkor said, his hand streaking over one of my breasts.

"Okay," I said breathily, my pulse picking up as his thumb teased my nipple.

"We should get back down before you make me lose control," Alkor said.

"Hey! I'm not doing anything!" I exclaimed. "You're the one doing things to me!"

"It is your fault for being so irresistible," he said, unrepentant. "You summon highly inappropriate thoughts to my mind considering our current venue. You must learn to behave."

I gaped at him only to have him smirk at me.

"Brace yourself, little temptress," Alkor said.

Before I could say a word, he took off flying again. This

time, despite the queasy feeling in the pit of my stomach, I kept my eyes wide open as we crossed the short distance to the trees.

"*Grack*," Alkor muttered.

"What is—" I started asking when his hand suddenly covered my mouth.

Alkor interrupted his descent only to climb back up. Pressing his lips to my ear, he whispered in an urgent voice. "Remain quiet, as still as possible, and as tightly aligned with my body as you can."

The hard edge to his voice betrayed his tension. Something had happened, but I didn't know what. Did someone take over our landing spot? I hadn't seen anyone in the trees, but then I'd been mostly focused on catching the last bird's eye view of the scenery. His hand released my mouth and wrapped around my waist, giving me greater support. My heart pounded, a million questions going off in my head as we flew alongside the trees towards a darker, less crowded area.

Alkor eventually seemed satisfied with one spot by a pond. We landed by tall bushes barely two meters behind a group of people fawning over a flock of lantern cranes propped up by the pond. It struck me as an incredibly risky location, but Alkor no sooner landed than he tucked away his wings and drew me by the hand closer to the group. One woman in the group turned to look at us, no doubt having heard our footsteps. She smiled politely then turned back to admire the scene.

Still reeling, I followed numbly as Alkor pulled me after him along the path towards the exit. I never felt when he disabled the camouflage. From the tension in his jaw, something had frazzled him. Curiosity and worry gnawed at me, but I didn't dare ask him any questions. Were we being followed? I didn't even dare to look behind or around us, not wanting to give away that we knew we had a tail if that were indeed the case.

In the end, we didn't leave the garden, but Alkor kept us in the midst of the largest clusters of people. I knew then beyond a doubt that he was trying to hide us in the crowd.

"Do you want to go home?" I asked, softly.

His golden eyes flicked towards me, guilt and worry mingling within. "You haven't seen everything," Alkor said sheepishly.

"No, but I've seen plenty. I don't mind," I said in a soft voice. "I have enough pictures for the project, and we can grab a few more on the way out."

"Are you sure?"

I nodded and smiled. Alkor smiled back, a grateful glimmer in his eyes. He gently kissed my forehead, wrapped an arm around my waist and then we headed toward the exit. As we passed a giant set of battling Samurai lanterns, the sudden impression of being observed hit me hard. The nervous tick along Alkor's jaw told me he felt it, too. Forcing myself to focus on the scene, I took a couple more pictures, and then we moved on.

The sensation of being followed remained with me until we reached the parking lot where I'd left my car. While I retrieved my keys from the clerk, Alkor looked inconspicuously around us. I couldn't wait to get inside the car to ask what the hell was going on. By the time we entered the vehicle, he seemed livid.

I opened my mouth the minute we each closed our doors.

"Not yet," Alkor whispered, trying to look discreetly through the rearview and side mirrors.

I bit my tongue, annoyed, stressed, and very freaked out. I started the car and drove off. Alkor launched into small talk about the exhibit we'd just attended, although he kept glancing at the mirrors, looking increasingly frustrated. My own irritation at not knowing what the fuck was going on had me on the verge of screaming. It was almost ten minutes into the drive before he finally seemed to relax.

"I'm sorry, Brianna," Alkor said, looking deflated. "This is not how I had envisioned our first evening out."

"What happened?" I asked, casting him a sideways glance, wishing I weren't driving right now.

"I believe members of the Rose Syndicate were following us," Alkor said in a somber tone. "They are a fanatic organization—almost a cult—that are determined to capture me and my people, to study us, experiment on us, and of course, to steal our technology."

"The Rose Syndicate?" I asked, even more freaked out.

"They have been hunting us for centuries. While it had been easier to avoid them in the past, the more that human technology evolves, the harder it becomes to fool them."

"Is that why you never leave the club?" I asked.

"Among other things."

"But..." I couldn't think straight. Too many questions battled to take control of my tongue. "What makes you think it's them? How do they know who... what you are?"

"It's not the first time I've tangled with them. They had captured two of my brothers before, and almost caught me on a few occasions. They've left me alone for a few years. It cannot be a coincidence that they show up now."

For the first time, I welcomed the light turning red on my approach. I stopped the car and turned to look at him.

"Why?" I asked. "Why are they showing up now? Does it have to do with whatever you're after in that room?" I'd taken a wild guess, but the way he stiffened confirmed I'd struck a nerve. His reluctance pissed me off. "Listen, I realize you're careful about revealing your secrets and shit, but I'm kind of involved right now. I think you owe me some explanation. Why am I really clearing that room for you? What do these guys want? What are you really? I mean, where do you come from? Are you sure you're not from the Underworld or some other dimension? And where does that camouflage technology come from?"

The light turning green only angered me further. I resumed driving, itching to just pull up somewhere and park the car to give him the third degree. But until I had a better understanding of how much of a threat those Rose Syndicate people were, I wanted to get our asses off the street.

"Like I previously told you, I'm a Khargal. And no, we do not come from the Underworld. As far as I know, there is no such thing," Alkor said cautiously.

"So where do you come from then?" I insisted.

Alkor took in a deep breath and exhaled loudly. "I come from a planet called Duras."

My jaw dropped, and I turned to stare at him, disbelieving.

"Look at the road!" Alkor exclaimed, straightening the wheel.

The car in the right lane honked at me. My stomach dropped, and my head snapped back towards the road. Heart pounding, I moved the car back to the center of my lane and focused on driving, my knuckles going white from holding the steering wheel so tightly.

I wanted to pull over, to get a grip on myself, and to gather my thoughts. But with the entrance of the Tunnel Ville-Marie looming ahead, stopping was no longer an option. Taking a few deep breaths, I flexed my fingers which had started hurting from clenching the wheel.

"I heard you say you came from some planet," I said, my voice trembling. "As in, you're an alien?"

"Is it that much more fantastic than the idea I could come from some kind of hell or underworld?" Alkor asked softly.

No. I guess not. But aliens didn't look like gargoyles. They looked like little grey men, with big ass eyes. Like E.T. or Thor... Well, okay, Thor and Superman were just pretty humans with godly powers. But aliens didn't look like gargoyles. Everyone knew that.

"But... How did you get here?"

"I'm not sure we should discuss this while you're driving," Alkor said, carefully.

"TELL ME!" I shouted, slapping the steering wheel.

Yeah, I was freaking out big time. And he was probably right about waiting until we got back to the club because I just knew he would drop another crazy bomb—or two—on me.

Alkor sighed, but complied. "Our spaceship crashed. My home world, Duras, was stuck in a never-ending war over the resources of a small, neighboring planet. Our government had sent us out on an exploratory mission to find another source for them. Our long range scans had indicated that one of the planets in your solar system might have what we needed. But when we came out of the wormhole that brought us here, we were hit by a solar flare."

Alkor rubbed his horns, a nervous gesture I'd seen him perform a couple of times before. Due to the human disguise his perception filter still displayed, he appeared to be rubbing thin air.

"So you were coming to plunder Earth's resources when you got struck down?" I said, my voice rising in pitch, already picturing some crazy alien invasion.

"No," Alkor said with a soft laugh. "Earth was never our destination. Mars was. The Prime Directive forbade us from landing on Earth to begin with. If not for that accident, we would have never made contact."

"Oh wow. You mean Prime Directive like in Star Trek?" I asked while taking the downtown exit ramp of the tunnel. "Like no talking or showing yourself to primitive species?"

Alkor chuckled again. "I wouldn't have worded it quite that way, but yes, that's the general idea."

"Wait a minute," I said, suddenly struck by a thought. "Was your crash what started that whole Roswell, Area 51 business?"

Alkor burst out laughing. "No, definitely not. Although many Khargals have grey skin, it was a different race of grey men that started that mess."

"So aliens do come to Earth? I mean, besides you guys," I added.

He nodded. "Well, besides a couple of crashes with no survivors—as far as I know—we are only aware of a few other alien species doing flybys, but also observing the Prime Directive."

My mind was reeling. I'd never believed humans to be alone in the universe. It always struck me as pretty egotistical to think that, out of hundreds of millions of stars, each with their own set of planets, ours would have been the only one to have produced life. But to have it confirmed, to be sitting next to an alien and, worse still, to have had wild, monkey sex with one…

Good God!

But then, come to think of it, Roswell didn't make sense. That incident took place in the late 1940s. Alkor would be ancient if he had arrived then. I cast a subtle glance in his direction, giving him a quick once over before turning my eyes back to the road.

Despite his disguise, which changed his face and the color of his skin, his body was the same. And what a body he possessed! Firm and muscular, he was a prime example of a fitness model. The memory of his hard skin against mine, his strong, bulging arms embracing me while he took me with unbridled passion had me hot and bothered in a blink.

Definitely nothing ancient about him.

"If you didn't crash in Roswell, when and where did you get here?"

Alkor shifted on his seat, his slight hesitation making me instantaneously suspicious.

"A while ago," he answered noncommittally.

"What does that mean specifically," I insisted, confused as to why he would dance around something like that. What could be more shocking than him being an alien? "I know it's been at least twenty years since you saved my life."

"Indeed," Alkor said, his voice taking on a wistful edge as he reminisced. "You were just a wisp of a girl. According to the Prime Directive, I shouldn't have interfered, but I couldn't just sit by while you died." He turned to look at me, an apologetic expression on his face. "I'm sorry about your mother. She was already beyond help."

"It's okay," I said with a stiff smile. "I know there's nothing you could have done. They said she died on impact, so at least she didn't suffer."

It wasn't okay. It would never be okay. Even after all this time, the loss of my mother still hurt. She'd been too young, too full of life to have been taken so brutally from us. But I didn't want to dwell on that now. Mom was never coming back.

"Don't think I haven't noticed how you changed the topic," I said, pulling up to the underground parking near the club.

"Right," Alkor said. "I apologize. I do not mean to be evasive. But I would rather we be back home to discuss this, without you being distracted by driving and away from prying eyes and ears. I will tell you everything. Just not here."

Fair enough. We were home already anyway.

Did I just think 'home'?

This wasn't home, but his place. And after this talk, I didn't know where our relationship would stand, if at all.

7

ALKOR

Brianna sat on the three-cushion couch, her gaze weighing heavily on me as I paced the room. It wasn't just the Prime Directive that made me uncomfortable revealing all to her. I'd already trampled all over that, but the more I revealed, the more I put her and the others in jeopardy. However, if I wanted her to come with me, I had to tell her everything.

"We crashed here a very, very long time ago," I said cautiously.

"As in?" she asked.

"As in a thousand years ago."

Brianna's jaw dropped, and her eyes bulged as she stared at me, speechless. "You mean your ancestors crashed which is why your numbers have dwindled so much, correct? Not *you* crashed, right?"

"No Brianna. *I* was part of the original crew."

She stared at me for a beat longer then jumped to her feet.

She marched towards one of the windows overlooking the park behind the church and hugged herself.

"Just how old are you?" she whispered, her back to me.

"I'm 1348 years old."

She slowly turned to look at me, flabbergasted. I shrugged, an apologetic expression on my face—although I didn't quite know why I felt the need to apologize.

"At least I don't sparkle in the sun?" I said, trying to lighten the mood.

She gave me 'the look' and shook her head. "Are you immortal?"

"No," I said advancing a couple steps of towards her. I hated the distance between us. "Khargals have an average lifespan of 3000 of your solar years."

"Fuck me..." she breathed out, running a nervous hand through her hair.

I almost said 'sure, right away' but thought better of it.

"You are way too old for me," Brianna whispered.

That struck a nerve. "No, I'm not. If we compare our overall lifespans that would make me about 45 years old."

"That's still a bit old compared to my 28," Brianna mumbled, although she seemed to be coming to terms with it. "Anyway, go on."

"Our ship crashed in the Bay of Biscay, off the coast of France. We couldn't have stumbled on a worse place; the seas are extremely rough over there and Khargals aren't exactly great swimmers. We're stone. Two-thirds of our crew died—including all of the females on board—some on impact, others from drowning. Unfortunately, our arrival didn't go unnoticed," I said, resuming my pacing. "The humans took us for demons and naturally sought to eliminate us. It became clear that remaining together would draw too much attention so we decided to split up and go into hiding while waiting to be rescued."

"A rescue that never came," Brianna said, with an air of sympathy.

"Never," I said, with a heavy sigh. "We didn't truly expect one either. Our beacon was lost in space before we breached Earth's atmosphere. Without it, there was no way for our signal to reach Duras. Somehow, the beacon must have fallen to Earth and gotten repaired."

"How do you know that?" Brianna asked. Before I could answer, her eyes narrowed as she put the pieces together. "Does it have to do with that room?"

I nodded. "Each of us have a sigil. It's a multi-function device, one of which is acting as a teleporter."

"Teleporter as in a 'beam me up, Scotty' type of thing?" Brianna asked.

I couldn't help a smile. "Yes. I have a psychic link to it. The minute the beacon became active, it sent a distress signal to Duras. The moment they answered, the sigil went online, and I felt it. A rescue team is on the way, but I need my sigil to know the rendezvous point, and for them to be able to teleport me to the ship."

Brianna stared at me quietly, visibly trying to hide her thoughts and feelings. "So... after a thousand years stranded on a primitive world, you finally get to go home," she said in a tone that failed to be as casual as she'd intended.

"Yes," I said softly.

"Congratulations," she said.

Despite the kindness of her words, her stiff posture, her

nails digging into her palms and her clenched jaw broadcast the anger seething beneath the surface.

"You knew you'd be leaving soon when you hired me," Brianna said, her voice taking on a harder edge.

"Yes. And you want to know why I'd get involved with you now after avoiding you for years?" I asked, although it wasn't actually a question.

"Lana could have handled it all," Brianna said bitterly. "Why reveal yourself and give me hope there might be something special between us when you knew this was going nowhere? Did you just want to get some last minute human pussy on your way out?"

I frowned at the crudeness of her words, but especially that she would think so little of me. My eyes boring into hers, I closed the distance between us. She lifted her chin defiantly and stood her ground.

"I revealed myself to you because the sigil going off changed everything." I advanced by a couple more steps, invading her personal space. Her breath caught, but she didn't back away. "I have pined after you for more than nine years."

Her lips parted, and her eyes widened.

"The first time we met, you were just a child in need of assistance," I said, placing my hands on her hips. "The second time, you were a young woman chasing after a memory. The minute you entered the club, my mating instincts awakened and went into overdrive. In over 1339 years of life, it had never happened, until you."

"And you said nothing?" I whispered.

"Prime Directive," I answered. "I'm a career soldier, Brianna. I follow rules. And even if I had wanted to break them, what kind of a future would I be condemning you to?

You would have to come live in hiding with me, and so would our offspring, if we ever had any. Do you have any idea how much I ached and hungered for you all those times you came knocking, seeking an audience with me?"

Wrapping an arm around her waist, I drew her to me, my other palm cupping her face. I examined her beautiful features that had haunted so many of my dreams and that would have kept me company had I gone into *duramna*, the deep sleep in stone form of the Khargals.

"What... What are mating instincts?" Brianna asked, her breathing coming in shorter bursts.

"It is a physical reaction when we meet the one being we are meant to spend the rest of our lives with. It gives me the urge to bite you when we are intimate, to bind you to me."

Her gaze lowered to my lips as if she could see my fangs through the skin. She shuddered, goosebumps erupting all over her skin. I brushed her hair from her face, my hand then resting on her nape.

"But you didn't bite me."

I shook my head. "No, because when I do, my mating glands will release certain chemicals that will pass into your system through the bite's venom, my saliva, and my semen. It will not turn you into a Khargal, but it will pass on to you some of our abilities."

Her eyes widened, curiosity, fear, and excitement shining within in equal measure.

"Such as?"

I smiled and let my thumb caress the gentle curve of her neck. "It will extend your lifespan, make you stronger, more resistant to injuries, quicker to heal, and make us compatible so that we could have offspring if we so wished."

"Wow! That sounds like rather good news."

I nodded, my smile broadening.

"But wait, that means I can't get pregnant from you right now?"

"Correct."

"Oh. So much for buying condoms and renewing my pills," Brianna mumbled under her breath.

"We don't need any of that," I said, leaning in to kiss her.

The softness of her lips beneath mine sent a surge of lust directly to my groin. The power she held over me was terrifying. I'd never felt so hungry for anything or anyone. Tilting my head to the side to deepen the kiss, I pressed her pliant body to mine, wanting greater proximity to my woman.

"No," Brianna said, breaking the kiss.

I looked at her, confused, as she pulled out of my embrace.

"You're leaving," she said. Sorrow and loss etched on her face, she took a couple of steps away from me.

I nodded. "Yes, I am. But I wish for you to come with me."

She pressed a hand to her chest as if to keep her heart from escaping.

"I had wanted us to grow a little closer over the next few days before I made this offer to you. But now that the Rose Syndicate has forced the issue, here we are."

I spoke in a lighthearted tone, but deep down, my stomach knotted painfully with fear that she might reject me. It was too much to expect of her so early in our relationship.

"Here we are," she repeated, a troubled expression on her face. "I'm guessing going to your world means no coming back to Earth, right?"

I shook my head with a sympathetic look.

She exhaled a shuddering breath and walked towards the window to look at the couples and tourists strolling in the park.

"That's a lot to digest," she said with forced laughter.

I carefully approached Brianna, standing inches from her back, but without making physical contact. I ached to touch her, hold her, but didn't want to push further. She leaned back, pressing her back to my chest. My arms immediately closed around her waist. I inhaled the lavender scent of her hair and gently kissed the top of her head.

"There is no rush, for now. You still have time to think about it."

She turned around in my arms, her eyes flicking between mine, searching. "But you were in a hurry to clear the room in the catacombs," she challenged.

"Yes, but only because I need to find out where the rendezvous point is and the pick-up date. For all I know, it could be somewhere in Africa, or Asia, that may require visas or vaccines to travel. Alone, I can easily work around most of these hurdles. But I'm hoping *not* to travel alone," I said, giving her a meaningful glance.

She smiled, although it was slightly uneasy. Brianna liked that I wanted her with me but obviously needed time to sort how she felt about such a venture. I just needed her to let her guard down enough for me to continue to woo her until it became obvious to her as well that she belonged by my side.

We spent the next couple of hours talking, with her giving me the third degree, wanting to know everything about my life on Earth over the past millennium, as well as any detail I felt comfortable giving about my fellow Khargals.

By the time I started describing the harsh world that was Duras, her eyelids had begun to droop. She'd had a long day's work, and tonight's emotions had wiped her out. I helped Brianna undress—although she kept her underwear—and tucked her into bed. In light of the strength of my lingering arousal, I didn't trust myself to lie next to her. In mere moments, her breathing deepened as she fell into a peaceful slumber.

I allowed myself a few minutes to gaze upon her beauty before climbing onto the pedestal I had moved back to my room. Perched on it, facing the East window so the rising sun would caress my face as it rose, I let myself enter *duramna*. My skin hardened, turning to stone. I didn't want to go too deep into it, like when I went into hibernation, but I needed to regenerate some of the energy I had spent earlier flying around with Brianna in the garden. My energy had drained too fast, proof that the lack of rigorous military training I'd been used to had taken its toll. The deeper I went into *duramna*, the faster I regenerated or healed if wounded.

Over the next few days, before we set out for the rendezvous point, I would spend every spare moment training to whip my stamina back into shape. If the need arose for me to fly with Brianna in my arms over long distances, I would need as much energy as possible.

⚜

This morning, after Brianna left for work, my first order of business had been to reinforce the security system of the club and to warn Lana to be on the lookout for any suspicious people lurking around the club, especially anyone with a ring, a pin or necklace with a rose on it. It also worried me that Brianna had been seen with me in a clearly romantic setting. I feared they might go after her to use her against me. Lana came from a far too influential family and was too much in the public eye to be trifled with. Any attack against her would bring about the exact type of scrutiny that the Rose Syndicate had always meticulously avoided. But if Brianna disappeared tomorrow, few people would notice. And those who did wouldn't have the kind of pull necessary to aid her or put pressure on the Syndicate.

She's far too easy prey.

We had agreed to have dinner at her place tonight. She wanted to cook for me, which I found endearing. I wondered what she'd say if I told her that instead of the pecan pie she intended to prepare for dessert, I would have preferred a few stones or plaster, for the nutrients, essential to a Khargal's diet, they contained.

I waited to sneak out of the club until Lana went to greet the delivery guys bringing the restaurant's fresh produce, meats, and beverages. She knew to leave the door wide open so that I could exit in stealth mode. My perception filter had been set to a different human visage. Unfortunately, it couldn't create a viable illusion of a shorter height unless you avoided any physical contact that would break the holographic display. With my 6'7, it was hard to be inconspicuous.

As per my routine whenever I snuck out of the club, I headed to one of the public bathrooms in the underground city, a network of shopping malls and connecting corridors that allowed you to cross the near entirety of downtown Montreal without ever having to set foot outside. I never used the same one twice, and would enter a stall in the quietest one only to come back out with my stealth device deactivated.

Blending in with the crowd, I hopped in a cab which I had drop me off in the general neighborhood of Brianna's house. I couldn't use my camouflage device to stealth around for extended periods as it drained much faster than my perception filter. Once again, I envied the Khargal scouts who could blend at will with the environment. To my relief, as I casually strolled towards my woman's house, I didn't detect any suspicious presence. Nevertheless, I remained cautious as I entered the building and used the spare key Brianna had given me to let myself in.

The spacious apartment reminded me of her. Subdued colors, peaceful yet inviting, with elegant furniture, delicate in appearance, but made of sturdy material. Although sparsely decorated, each element was meaningful, intriguing, and told a story that piqued the curiosity. Forcing myself to focus on the task at hand, I upgraded her security system with new, state of the art locks, a camera system that she had full control over, and which covered every access into the apartment.

Brianna arrived just as I was testing the various settings of the system. She didn't give me a chance to free her from her burden of grocery bags, discarding them instead on the console in the entrance. My woman closed the distance between us, wrapping her arms around my neck. I lowered my head to capture her lips, purring with pleasure at the exquisite taste of her.

I could get used to this.

To welcome my mate home after work, or for her to greet me upon my return like this, painted a pleasant picture. As the kiss deepened, Brianna's fingers found their way through my hair, and rubbed the skin at the base of my short horns, seven in total. She'd discovered how sensitive it was, especially around the three at the center top of my head. My cock jerked in my pants, blood rushing to my groin, making it stiffen. The mating glands at the back of my throat swelled, demanding once again that I bind my mate. I swallowed hard, refusing to give in to the burning temptation.

Pulling my woman's hands away from my horns, I freed her of her trench coat and slipped my hand beneath her blouse, seeking the rounded mounds of her breasts and the hard buttons of her nipples. Brianna whisked her blouse over her head and discarded it with a flick of her wrist, before fiddling with the waist of my pants, trying to lower them. I didn't resist, too focused on unclasping her bra. Those wretched things were created to drive a man insane. How women managed to attach and detach them with such ease boggled my mind.

Just as I succeeded, Brianna dropped to her knees before me and greedily took my cock in her mouth. I hissed with pleasure, my hands fisting in her hair. The warmth of her lips around me, her tongue licking, and her teeth grazing the sensitive skin of my shaft, had a pool of lava swirling in the pit of my stomach. My hips moved in counterpoint to her movements as she deep throated me. I felt guilty that my woman should pleasure me before I had made her climax, but Brianna seemed to love going down on me—not that I complained. She'd become addicted to my taste, salty caramel she called it. But I didn't want to find my release in her mouth. I wanted my seed inside her, with her inner walls clamping down on my cock while she screamed my name in ecstasy.

With a deep moan, I forced myself away from her grasp.

She looked up at me in surprise when I forced her up on her feet and pushed her against the wall. I kissed her, my tongue invading her mouth while my fingers feverishly unzipped her skirt. It fell to the floor with the bristling sound of fabric.

This time, it was my turn to drop to my knees, kissing my way down her neck, stopping to pay homage to her breasts, and for my tongue to tickle her navel before feasting on her burning core. Brianna's back arched off the wall as a strangled cry tore out of her. The scent of her arousal made my cock throb with the need to possess her, the taste of her essence the most divine nectar on my tongue. According to my woman, its rougher texture stimulated her in the most delicious way. I therefore made it a point to give her sensitive clit a proper tongue lashing while my fingers dipped inside her wet opening.

I loved how responsive Brianna always was to my touch. I crooked my fingers inside of her, grazing her sensitive spot, and she fell apart, shouting my name. Legs trembling, she nearly collapsed. Slipping my arms under her knees, I lifted her up against the wall and rammed my aching cock deep inside her. She shouted again, still riding the waves of her orgasm as I began pounding in and out of her.

"*Grack!*" I cussed as the spasms of her inner walls around my shaft tried to force out a climax that I wasn't ready to welcome just yet.

She felt too damn good, stroking my cock with each thrust, her burning skin against mine, her hands clawing at me, her labored breath fanning over my chest.

"Touch yourself," I ordered without slowing my punishing pace.

Obedient, Brianna slipped a shaky hand between us and

started rubbing her clit. Her eyes almost immediately rolled into the back of her head as another orgasm descended upon her, squeezing my own release from me. I rocked in and out of her at a much slower pace until the last of my seed was spent.

Leaning against her, I suddenly realized that my wings had come out. Pushing away from the wall, I wrapped them around her, sheltering my female. Brianna's head resting on my shoulder, my cock still buried inside her, I slowly, carefully walked us to the bathroom. With much reluctance, I opened my wings, pulled out my cock, and set my woman on her feet so that we could shower together.

When we finished, she let me dry her. The look in Brianna's eyes as she gazed upon me held such tenderness, affection, and wonder that hope blossomed in my heart that when the time to choose came, she would pick me.

I almost panicked upon waking in Brianna's bed, the unfamiliar surroundings throwing me for a loop. The little minx laughed at my disoriented look. I felt pathetic being so easily fazed. As a warrior, I should be on top of my game at all times. But I guess a millennium out of service would dull anyone's reflexes.

Just like Lana, when Brianna invited you to dinner, she cooked for an entire army. My stomach still bulged from the previous night's overindulgence. She had packed a few containers of leftovers for me to bring home for lunch and to share with Lana. I didn't mind, considering her food had been delicious. I simply didn't tell her that I'd snuck out to eat a few rocks during the night. There would be time to explain that later.

With a heavy heart, I watched my female leave for work. To my chagrin, Brianna didn't need to be at the club while the workers cleared the debris, and other tasks awaited her at the office. How quickly I'd become addicted to her presence, to the sexy sound of her voice, and the affectionate way in which she constantly touched me, as if to reassure herself of my presence.

I still couldn't believe how well Brianna had taken all my revelations, once she'd overcome her initial shock. Humans didn't have Khargal mating instincts, and yet she couldn't deny feeling a strong, quasi irrational, attraction towards me. I wanted to believe something deeper than sexual tension motivated her. Real chemistry existed between us. But with me semi-trapped in my club, it added an extra burden to our efforts to build on an already unorthodox relationship. As much as discovering the distance that existed between her and her father had upset me for her sake, it pleased me now to the extent that she'd be less likely to want to stay on Earth for him.

Once I brought her onboard the rescue ship, there would, no doubt, be quite a few frowns. I might even face disciplinary measures for violating the Prime Directive. But then my friendship with Lana, who would be staying here, had also been a violation. Pretty much every single one of the surviving Khargals had formed a special bond of friendship with a human that assisted us in one form or another with living on Earth. Whatever the punishment, I would accept it as long as they didn't dare try to take my woman from me. I didn't really fear that would be the case though. Khargals respected the sacred bond that existed between true mates.

Forcing my thoughts back to more productive endeavors, I called my notary to give my approval on the final draft of my revised will. He confirmed the official documents would be couriered to me today. I'd have to ask Lana to call her friend, the Commissioner of Oaths, to bear witness when I signed. After hanging up, I cast a vague glance at the monitors displaying different angles of the room being cleared, only to do a double-take. I jumped to my feet, my eyes widening at the sight of the gargoyle face carved into the wall that had finally been revealed.

I raced to the catacombs and called on Stephen, the construction manager, to tell him to halt the work for the day. With the sigil within reach, I wanted everyone out in order to open the secret cache without prying eyes in the vicinity.

He argued at first, saying there was still some debris left to be removed in the room and, with their current progress, they could get started on the second room two days early. My impatience to see them all leave must have been evident in the curtness of my response. Frowning in confusion, Stephen gave me a stiff nod and then proceeded to herd his men out of the catacombs.

No sooner had the last man left than I headed for the gargoyle face carved into the wall. After a century of disuse, and the collapse from the explosion, I prayed that the opening mechanism of the secret cache remained functional. Releasing my claws, I used their sharp tips to dislodge some of the dirt around the hidden switches. The bulging eyes of the gargoyle would have been too obvious. Instead, the switches were concealed in the spiraling ornaments surrounding the face.

Two specific spots, with nothing in common visually, needed to be depressed simultaneously, the pressure applied for at least five seconds before the mechanism released. It ensured no one would reveal it by accident. Even if someone tried to open it, if they didn't know exactly how, chances were they would never find it.

A victorious growl rose from my throat as the grinding sound of stone against stone echoed in the empty room. The gargoyle face slid to the side, revealing a gaping, recessed shelf behind it. Plumes of dust rose around the face, and small rocks drizzled to the ground. I waved the dust away, then held my hand before the scanner, invisible to human eyes, so that it could identify my digital prints. Once again, it took a little over five seconds for the blue laser to appear and scan my palm. The delay was meant to fool a potential intruder into a false sense of safety, causing him to trip the booby trap.

As soon as the scanner chimed, confirming the trap was disabled, I reached for the sigil, ignoring the couple of other devices I had hidden here. My brain tingled from the psychic connection with the sigil. No bigger than a medallion, the device fit snugly in the palm of my hand. It immediately responded to contact with my DNA. The large, red gem in its center lit up, bathing the entire room in a bright, red glow. With a small flash, a 3D hologram of a mountain appeared above the sigil. Floating next to it, script text written in Durassian indicated the pick-up time and date, the name of the mountain range, and its coordinates.

My heart soared, and my throat tightened with emotion. Despite my conviction that the sigil had indeed become active, until this instant, a doubt had lingered in the back of my head that maybe I'd imagined it all. But now, I held irrefutable proof that, at long last, we were going home.

With my free hand, I rotated the holographic representation of the mountain. The rendezvous point had been set to Mount Nirvana in the Canadian Northwest Territories. Zooming in, the mountain face didn't show any roads or easy access. This would be a tough climb—an impossible climb for a novice—or an easy flight for a Khargal. I would need to train hard to be able to carry Brianna over such a long distance. Thankfully, the pick-up date was set for October 31st. That still left me three weeks to get back in shape and convince my woman she belonged with me.

Turning off the sigil, I shoved it into my pocket and reached for my armor and the defective weapon which I had stashed away here. I'd barely raised my hand when a subtle sound had my head jerking back to look over my shoulder.

Grack!

How could I have let a damn human get the drop on me? That was twice now.

"Hands up where I can see them, creature!" the man said, leveling a dart gun unlike anything I'd ever seen before.

I pretended to comply, assessing the extent of the threat and turning my skin to stone. As I'd not deactivated my perception filter yet, he couldn't see my transformation, nor my wings opening. The challenge would be fighting with stone skin. It made us heavier and our movements slower, thus draining us faster of energy. If not careful, I could drain myself to the point of exhaustion, and become helpless in front of an enemy.

"What is the meaning of this?" I asked, playing dumb.

And then it struck me. "I know you! You're one of the workers. You're here to rob me?"

"Do not take me for a fool," the man said in a sharp tone laced with a subtle British accent. "You know exactly what I am, just like I know what kind of abomination you are."

My eyes flicked to his hand wielding the gun, and my stomach dropped as I recognized the ring with the symbol of a rose adorning his finger.

His lips stretched into a malicious smile as he noticed where my gaze had wandered. He wiggled his fingers, flaunting the ring.

"I see you're familiar with it," the man said. "Good, we can get straight to business. You have something we want. Hand it over and don't make a fuss. Give me a hard time, and that human traitor you're fucking will have a most unpleasant time."

My blood froze in my veins, and an angry haze descended before my eyes. I advanced by one menacing step towards him.

"Hey!" the Rose Syndicate agent snapped. "You stay right where you are or I'll pump you full of drugs. I don't give a shit if you overdose. We already have another one of you monsters for our studies. We don't need you alive. We just want that thing in your pocket. So hand it over."

"*Lar* forsakes you, vermin!" I hissed before rushing him.

He fired his gun, the dart glancing off the side of my wing as I veered right to dodge it. Standing his ground, he fired three more times in quick succession. I swatted the first dart out of the way and barely managed to dodge the second one, my movements significantly slowed down by the heaviness of stone form. But the third found its mark in my shoulder.

Although I immediately yanked it out, numbness began to spread.

How in Lar's name had the dart pierced through my stone skin?

Whatever substance it had contained, it would soon have me completely incapacitated. Throwing caution to the wind, I charged him only to have another dart hit me square in the chest while the agent quickly backed away from me. The dart's vile content immediately coursed through me, making my legs wobble and my stomach churn.

Stone skin had been a mistake.

Without it, I would have been faster. Even if he had shot me a second time, he'd be lying on the ground with a broken neck right now. Until this instant, piercing rounds were the only type of human ammunitions that had worried me as they punched through our stone skin to bite into our flesh. But these darts…

The man took aim again and I brought my right wing before me to shield myself. He fired but his dart gun clicked empty. I spread my wing open to clear my line of sight only to find the man fumbling with his pocket. His face drained of blood, proper fear descending upon him when our eyes connected, and I shed my stone skin. I stumbled towards the doorway, my vision blurring and my limbs getting heavy. And yet, even with the drug on the verge of overwhelming me, we both knew he wouldn't escape me.

The man yanked out of his pocket a small device that resembled a remote car key and pressed a button on it. A series of quick snapping sounds resonated overhead, no louder than firecrackers going off. I raised my head just in time to see a series of large stones collapsing on me. The brutal impact knocked me to my knees.

I'd grown too numb to push off the boulder that had fallen over my wing.

"If you want what's in my pocket," I slurred, "come and get it."

The man snarled, realizing he'd effectively blocked his own access to my right pocket with the boulder pinning my wing down against my side. If he were dumb enough to approach, I'd claw his face off. And once I lost consciousness, my body would enter *duramna*. My Durassian pants would turn to stone as well, further sheltering the sigil from his filthy hands.

"You will bring us the medallion, or the little engineer won't be so pretty anymore," the man said, regaining his cocky attitude. "You will receive your instructions soon. Do not disappoint us."

As darkness descended before my eyes, another series of snapping sounds brought the collapse of more rocks and boulders, this time completely sealing me inside the room.

A single name occupied my last thought.

Brianna.

❧ 8 ❧

BRIANNA

My phone rang, breaking my concentration. The number didn't look familiar.

"Hello?" I answered.

"Ms. Brent?" asked a male voice I didn't know.

"Speaking."

"My name is Charles Lumney, one of the workers at The Darkest Hour."

My stomach dropped, a sudden sense of impending doom washing over me.

"I'm sorry, Madam, but there's been a terrible accident," the man said in a commiserating voice. "Part of the hallway has collapsed. Stephen and Mr. Drayvus both got severely injured. The first responders are on the way. I think you should come, too."

"Oh my God!" I exclaimed. Jumping to my feet, I grabbed my purse from my desk drawer. In my haste, I almost upended it. "How bad is it?" I asked, running towards the elevators.

"It's hard to tell, Ms. Brent," the man said, sounding

deflated. "They're both stuck under the rubble, and there's a lot of blood pooling from under there."

"Oh God!" I felt dizzy with fear, imagining the worst. "Marnie, there's been an incident on one of the construction sites. I don't know when I'll be back," I shouted to the receptionist, not waiting for her answer as I jumped into an open elevator by the reception desk. "I'm on my way, Mr. Lumney," I said back into my phone. "Everything will be okay."

"All right, thank you, Ma'am."

The elevator doors closed as I continued to frantically punch the button to the underground parking of the building. I eventually stopped when the lift started moving, berating myself for doing exactly what I hated seeing other people do whenever they entered an elevator. I tried to call Lana but there was no signal in the lift. Stomach in knots, I couldn't breathe at the thought that something terrible could have happened to Alkor. But worse still, what would happen when they removed the stones he was trapped under and saw his true appearance? Would they even know how to heal a Khargal?

The lift finally reached its destination. When the door opened at last, I skip-ran to my car while once again trying to call Lana. But of course, the signal acted up as was often the case when in the underground garage. As I closed the distance to my car, a familiar-looking man approached me. I didn't have time to chitchat, but he called out my name, forcing me to slow down.

"Ms. Brent?" he man asked.

"I'm sorry, sir, but I'm in a hurry," I said without stopping.

"I know," the man said. "I've been sent to pick you up to drive you to The Darkest Hour. I'm one of the workers."

"Oh!" I said, stopping dead in my tracks. I was terrible at driving when under strong emotional turmoil. Come to think of it, I should have hopped in a cab instead. "Yes. Yes, thank you. That would be great."

"This way," he said with a pleased smile.

As we approached his vehicle, he unlocked the doors of a black sedan with the remote. I didn't know jack about cars but his seemed a tad fancy for a construction worker going on site. That first random thought raised an avalanche of other questions. Why had he come to pick me up? How did he know where I worked when he was Stephen's contractual employee? How did he get here so fast? Why didn't Lumney warn me he had sent someone to get me?

My steps faltered, and I stopped a couple of feet from the car. The man, who had been opening the door to the driver's seat, paused and looked at me questioningly. My expression must have given away my sudden suspicions. His face hardened, losing all traces of his earlier kindness.

"Get your ass in the car, bitch, before I shoot you," he said in a menacing voice.

I gasped and stumbled two steps back. Before I could react, I watched the man pull the trigger on his strange gun. As if in slow motion, a dart flew towards me before embedding itself in my torso. The only sound I emitted could have passed for a hiccup before nauseating numbness spread through me. With an annoyed expression, the man circled around the car towards me just as I collapsed to the ground, lost in oblivion.

I regained consciousness, my wrists and ankles shackled to a chair in an interrogation room. The overly bright neon lights on the ceiling made the barren, pale grey walls appear white. I blinked until my vision cleared. Two empty chairs across the metal table in front of me were my sole companions. The clichéd two-way mirror didn't feature in the room but a camera in the top left corner probably took its place.

The clicking sound of the door opening startled me. Stephen and the 'construction worker' who had abducted me walked into the room. My chest tightened at the sight of the construction manager. We'd worked together for years. I'd grown to consider him a friend and even worried he was lying injured under the so-called collapse. What the hell was going on? I stared at him with disbelieving eyes as both men took a seat in the chairs across the table from me.

"Hello, Brianna," Stephen said, an apologetic hint in his dark-brown eyes. "It is unfortunate that we should meet again under these circumstances."

"What is going on, Stephen?" I asked, anger and betrayal burning through me. "Why am I here?"

"This is Daniel, my partner," Stephen said, ignoring my questions. "I've always had the utmost respect for you as an engineer and a professional. Our collaborations over the years have proven quite successful and provided me with the perfect cover during my investigations."

"Investigations?" I asked, a sense of dread rising in the pit of my stomach, already guessing where this was headed.

"You specialize in historical buildings, and you have done

your damnedest to secure every church project your firm contracted. That suited me perfectly. You see, like you, my organization seeks the stone creatures."

My involuntary sharp breath intake gave me away. Stephen's knowing smile confirmed I'd blown my chances of playing dumb.

"Your organization?" I asked, trying to change the course of the conversation.

"Almost twenty years ago, we came across an interesting police report which mentioned the delirious ramblings of a grieving little girl who had lost her mother in a car crash and barely survived drowning herself," Daniel said. "The poor child claimed a gentle, stone demon had rescued her and her dad from the sinking car. Naturally, the authorities dismissed that claim, but we knew better."

"We've been keeping a close eye on you ever since, in case your 'rescuer' would show up again," Stephen said, leaning against the back of his chair. "You've been impressive in your efforts to dig up information about the Creatures. We often considered offering you a chance to join our organization, but you have too romantic an idea of what they truly are. Until we knew if you would be a fit with us, I'd decided to collaborate with you on your various projects."

"You mean use me to try to get closer to them," I said bitterly.

"Semantics," Stephen said with a shrug, his face taking on a bored expression. "When Drayvus gave you the contract, and you reached out to us, I could have kissed you! Do you have any idea how long we've been trying to approach him to verify our suspicions that he was the real deal and not some freak cosplay fan?"

"What do you want from him?" I asked, anger fueled by my protective instincts towards Alkor seeping in to my voice. "He doesn't bother anyone, pays his taxes, and observes our laws. Why not just leave him alone?"

The look of pure contempt Stephen leveled me with made me shudder. This was not the man I had grown to believe a friend.

"You are a foolish girl. I'd expected better from you, to be honest. All he had to do was show you his wings for you to jump into bed with him. With *it*!" Stephen spat with disdain. "How could you lay with a monster?"

My face heated, but I lifted my chin defiantly. "The only monsters I see right now are sitting across this table from me. He saved my life when he had no reason to, exposing himself in the process. He had nothing to gain from it and never asked for anything in return. All these years, he's been an exemplary citizen. Why do you want to harass him now?"

Stephen shook his head in disappointment, his shoulder-length dark brown hair waving with each movement. "He played the long-game with you. Earned your loyalty, made you chase after him, staying just out of reach to keep you trying until he had you exactly where he wanted you. Until you were ripe for the picking."

My stomach knotted, an uneasy feeling blossoming deep within me at hearing him voice the fear that had haunted me ever since Alkor first revealed his true nature to me.

Stephen rested his ankle over his knee, his hands clasped in front of him. "Didn't you find it strange that he has finally agreed to see you when his sigil has become active?"

"He needed the help of a specialized architectural engineer, which I happen to be," I said defensively. "It's not really coincidence either since I deliberately went into this field in the hope something like this would happen."

"They called your firm specifically," Daniel interjected, "knowing *you* were the main expert in old churches. It is no accident you ended up there. This was planned."

Because I'm his soulmate. He wanted me there to give us an ultimate chance. Right?

I hated that they'd successfully planted the seed of doubt.

"All right, I'll bite," I said, trying to rein in my anger and hurt. "Why go through this elaborate scheme to get me? What do I have that he wants? What's his goal?"

"He wants a blindly devoted minion who will follow him to the end of the world while he's preparing an invasion."

I burst out laughing, realizing we'd just entered tin foil hat territory. "You're crazy," I blurted out.

"He's not," Daniel said, his pitch black eyes boring into me. A small scar I hadn't noticed on the right side of his chin stood out from his pale skin when he clenched his teeth. "The sigils are homing devices. Every single sigil whose location we knew of has gone active. The creatures that owned them are bending over backwards to recover them. We've gotten one of them to confess that the device served to call more of their kind here."

"To rescue them!" I exclaimed, bewildered. "It just sent out a distress signal! The Khargals want to go home. Wouldn't you in their shoes? They've been stranded here for centuries, forced to live in hiding. Of course they will want to go home, reunite with their loved ones, and go back to a normal life. Why do we always assume the worst of people?"

Stephen shook his head again, his disappointment plain to see. "They are not people. And this is why we never approached you. You're too soft. Those romantic ideals of yours could bring about the downfall of the human race. He has completely brainwashed you. We've extracted sufficient information from them to know they are a threat to us and to our future."

"Oh my God," I breathed out. "You've tortured them."

Stephen lifted his chin, his unrepentant gaze hardening. "We do what we must to protect mankind."

"The Inquisition, too, did what it thought was right to get people to confess. We all know that under sufficient pain, people will say anything for it to end, even admit to crimes they didn't commit."

"She's too far gone," Daniel said to Stephen like I wasn't sitting right there.

"Indeed," Stephen said with a sigh. "Such a disappointment. Such great potential wasted." He turned his dark-brown eyes towards me, all warmth and friendliness gone. "You will tell us everything you know about the sigil, their rendezvous point, and how big a fleet they have coming."

My back stiffened, and my blood turned to ice. The unforgiving expression in his eyes and the mad glint in Daniel's gaze as they both stared at me made me fear the worst. Made me fear the Inquisition.

"We can do this the easy way, or the hard way," Stephen said. "Either way, we will know everything you do."

I swallowed hard, my stomach clenching in fear when Daniel retrieved a small syringe from his shirt pocket and placed it on top of the table in front of us.

"What's that?" I asked, unable to hide the trembling in my voice.

"Something that will help you cooperate," Stephen said.

"I don't know anything!" I exclaimed. "He and I just met. You know everything I know, more even. He only told me that he needed the room cleared to recover his sigil and that would help him go back home. I swear, that's all I know."

"As you wish," Stephen said, nodding at Daniel to proceed.

"NO!" I shouted as Daniel rose to his feet, picked up the syringe and approached me. "Stephen, don't do this! I don't know anything else."

"We'll find out soon enough, won't we?" he said with a nonchalant shrug.

I pulled against my restraint in a futile effort to keep far away from my tormentor. The cold, hard metal of my shackles chafed the tender skin of my wrists. Daniel pressed his palm on my forearm, near the elbow, to temper my struggles. Seconds later, the pinching sensation of the needle sinking into my flesh was swiftly followed by a strange feeling of euphoria and peace.

My head felt a little heavy, and I couldn't quite hang on to the reason for my anger and fear. I blinked and looked at the reassuringly familiar face sitting across the table from me. Why was he just staring at me like some kind of strange phenomenon he wanted to study?

"How are you feeling, Brianna?" my friend Stephen asked.

"I'm doing great!" I said with a smile. "Well, mostly," I amended. "My head feels a little heavy, but good otherwise."

"Excellent. I'm happy to hear it," Stephen said, smiling back at me.

I liked it when he smiled. He reminded me of my father

back in the days when we were happy, when he still loved me, and called me his little princess.

"I need your help, Brianna. Do you want to help me?" he asked.

"Yes, of course! What can I do for you?"

"I would love for you to tell me anything you can about Alkor Drayvus. Any single detail, however insignificant," Stephen said with his usual, friendly… fatherly voice.

He'd shown me a picture of his daughter once. She was almost the same age as me and, in many ways, she actually looked like me. I remembered feeling some fierce, irrational jealousy.

"As you know, it's important for me to understand the psychology of a client if I am to do construction work for him."

"I'm not sure this construction is going to happen," I said with a sympathetic look.

"Why is that?" Stephen asked.

"Because Alkor is leaving in the next couple of weeks. He's going far away, and he's never coming back. But he wants me to go with him," I said with a grin. My mind wandered, reminiscing about the sweet way in which he cuddled with me and held me like I was the most precious thing in the world. "He says I'm the only woman to have ever awoken his mating instincts, even though he's been alive over 1300 years! He sure knows how to make a girl feel special."

I giggled thinking about how he said he wanted to bite me and exchange fluids with me.

Stephen and Daniel exchanged a look I didn't understand, but that too made me giggle. They then proceeded to ask me a million questions about Alkor and me. I didn't mind answering them although after a while, I started feeling a little uneasy about it. For some reason, I suspected Alkor wouldn't like me revealing some of the things that frankly felt rather private. And that damn pressure in my head that was borderline turning into a migraine wouldn't leave me alone.

At long last, they seemed satisfied and brought me to a room where I could nap to get rid of that migraine. Even as they escorted me there, it struck me as odd that I'd been shackled to the chair. But my brain refused to compute anymore. There would be time to reflect on all that later. For now, I just needed to sleep. The minute my head touched the pillow, the world ceased to exist and blessed oblivion claimed me.

9

ALKOR

I awoke beneath the rubble, livid, angry with myself for 'getting my butt handed to me' like the humans like to say, and by a weakling no less. But more importantly, I was furious to have put Brianna in jeopardy with my negligence. The rubble had done little damage to me. It took a lot to damage a Khargal. We weren't bulletproof, but unless they used armor piercing rounds—and even then—we could sustain a lot of hits before getting into real trouble when sheltered by our stone skin.

So, how in Lar's name had those damn darts not shattered against me on impact?

I knew that the Rose Syndicate had held a few Khargals captive, some for decades. Many of us, at various periods, had tried to rescue them only to find they'd been moved to a new, unknown location. Despite that and whatever experiments they no doubt performed on my brothers, the Rose Syndicate had never developed any technology that represented a serious threat against us, until now. What else had they created that we might be vulnerable to?

Grunting with effort, I pushed on the boulders pinning me to the ground. I had no idea how long I'd been out under the effects of that drug. As with any time I'd found myself in a position of vulnerability, I'd instinctively gone into *duramna*. The stone sleep had allowed me to regenerate a little and, in theory, to eliminate the drug from my system faster. Once I managed to shuffle the rocks sufficiently to have a bit of wiggle room, I brought a few small stones to my lips and ate them for an instant burst of energy and extra fuel.

Although still trapped under piles of rocks, I finally had enough room to retrieve my phone from my pants pocket. My relief at finding it intact was short lived as it didn't have any signal. In an excess of rage, I almost smashed it against the rocks imprisoning me, but thankfully, managed to rein in my temper. I needed to keep a cool head if I were to get out of there in one piece and in time to rescue my Brianna.

To my great distress, my phone indicated it was already 19:11. I'd been out for eight hours. Brianna should have been here already for our date. She would have asked Lana about me and, together, they would have figured out my predicament. That she hadn't come looking for me in the catacombs, after being unable to find me in my private quarters, confirmed my greatest fears.

Lana wouldn't start worrying about not hearing from me for at least 48 hours, especially now that I was involved with Brianna. And as I'd told the workers not to return until I informed them to do so, no one would show up tomorrow morning. I needed to get out of this on my own, and quickly.

It took a couple of hours to extract myself from the rubble.

Looking up at the ceiling, it was clear that the charges had been carefully placed for the trap, to create the largest collapse possible without threatening the integrity of the building. This kind of work couldn't have gone unnoticed by the construction manager. I therefore had to assume Stephen was in on it and likely a handful of the workers.

Racing up the stairs, I kept a close eye on my phone until the signal came back on. As soon as it did, I made to call Brianna but stopped; the club was in full swing, the loud music drowning out everything. The thumping of the base resonated all the way into my chest. I made a beeline for the elevator and noticed the unusually large number of stunned or baffled stares in my direction. I was used to drawing people's attention, but something else was happening here.

"*Grack!*" I muttered after casting a quick glance at my wrist bracer which controlled my perception filter. It pulsated an orange color indicating a malfunction.

Discarding my plan of climbing the stairs to my private quarters—which would have been faster—I threw myself inside the lift to hide from prying eyes. As soon as I entered my chamber, I groaned inwardly at my reflection in the mirror. The holographic disguise flickered in and out of existence, having me alternating between my Khargal form, wings on full display, and my human disguise.

So much for the Prime Directive.

At least, the stroboscope had been running when I crossed the room. Hopefully, most of the patrons would dismiss this as an optical illusion enhanced by the strobe lights.

Sheltered from the noise at last, I called Brianna and waited multiple rings without a response. Finally, someone picked up.

"Tomorrow, at 2300 hours, bring the medallion to the Belvedere," said the voice of the male who had attacked me in the catacombs. "Don't be late. If you fail to show up, we'll find out how well your woman can fly."

He hung up before I could reply. Of all the *gracking* vague messages! In Montreal, whenever someone said the Belvedere, it usually referred to one of four fairly busy areas on top of Mount Royal for locals and tourists alike to enjoy breathtaking views of the city. In the evenings, it constituted a common romantic getaway for couples.

Of the four Belvederes, only the Summit Circle one was easily accessible with a parking spot right at the belvedere. With a prisoner in tow, it seemed like the most viable one for them to go. Although it legally closed at 23:00, young party goers often gathered there after hours for beer and to do drugs. But I had no doubt the resourceful Rose Syndicate agents could figure out a way to keep them out to hold our little standoff.

I dismissed the Camilien-Houde Belvedere and the Kondiaronk Belvedere as both were always much too crowded and required quite a bit of walking to reach.

Despite the ten minute walk to reach the Outremont Belvedere, it struck me as the most likely choice. It didn't appear on any map of the city and no signs led to it. The view wasn't as stunning and few people would head there at night, having to travel a somewhat dark, woodsy trail.

As much as I hated having to wait nearly 24 hours before the meeting, which I'd spend worrying about Brianna's welfare, the delay gave me a much needed reprieve. Despite our enhanced strength in comparison to humans, we weren't herculean. Eating stones mostly provided quick healing and only minute bursts of energy. I needed to go into *duramna*, to fully regenerate and heal the bruises from getting pummeled by the fallen boulders, before I faced off against the fanatics of the Syndicate.

On the bright side, I had recovered my armor and my shield. Despite my weariness, I tested both to make sure they still functioned. The suit's embedded camouflage system would allow me to stealth past the Syndicate's agents. Much stronger than my mobile stealth device, it would hide Brianna more effectively once I recovered her.

However, my shield gave me a bit of a scare. But of course, it needed to be recharged after decades of disuse. The wrist attachment would deploy an energy field that could deflect or absorb most types of projectiles or energy blasts. The thought of those darts piercing my stone skin still had me spooked. Despite still being primitive by Durassian standards, humanity had come a long way technology-wise. Soon, they could prove to be a real threat.

I'd spent the past thousand years keeping a close eye on human technology, learning all that I could not only to be able to set up my own security systems, but also in the hopes maintaining, repairing or recreating some of our old Khargal technology. Too bad it still didn't allow me to fix my weapon.

My tasks completed, I once more settled on my perch, thoughts of Brianna keeping me company as I surrendered to the peaceful void of deep *duramna*.

I took a taxi, asking to be dropped off near one of the entrances of the Notre-Dame-des-Neiges cemetery. Ideally, I would have simply flown here, but not knowing what kind of enemy forces awaited me, it felt safer to preserve my energy as much as possible. As I entered the wooded area leading up to the secret lookout, I deactivated my perception filter, which had given me a casual human appearance. After activating the camouflage of the armor I wore, I summoned my wings, and then took flight.

I climbed higher than necessary so that I could glide over the Belvedere to assess the situation without the flapping of my wings giving away my position. As soon as I flew over the lookout, I realized my mistake. The place being vacant only further confirmed it. Although I knew of this area, I'd never visited it before. The lookout had no protective ramp or railings because the promontory didn't end in a cliff or edge with a sharp drop, but rather with a semi-steep incline. They couldn't push her off to her death. She'd only roll down the slope over a few meters before stopping.

Damn them all to Macero!

The Summit Circle Belvedere was located on the other side of the mountain. So much for preserving my energy. With an angry growl, I flapped my wings hard as I raced to the only other place that made sense… I hoped. At least, without my stone skin, I could fly for hours over very long distances before it began to take its toll. Thankfully, I had come forty minutes early for a chance at getting the drop on them. Even with the ten minute flight to reach the other side of Mount Royal, I arrived thirty minutes in advance at the lookout.

My heart soared at the sight of my mate, only to have that

elation replaced by anger. Stephen, holding her firmly by the upper arm, all but dragged her to the railing in front of the parking area. Shackled and visibly frightened, Brianna nodded submissively when he ordered her to stay put. Three of his men took position after securing the perimeter. Two more went to hide in the nearby wooded area, almost in sniper positions. With most of the trees having lost their leaves, they relied on the cover of darkness to avoid detection. That was stupid considering I had perfect night vision.

Signs along the road leading to the lookout indicated it was closed for the night due to a movie shooting. That explained the absence of straggling tourists or late night partiers. This made sense with Montreal having grown quite popular for shooting both blockbuster movies and TV series.

Gliding in a downward spiral, I landed quietly near the two cars of the Rose Syndicate agents. I whipped out my claws and slashed their rear tires. Moving quickly, but silently, I prowled after one of the two snipers, thankful for the absence of snow and for the dry ground so that I didn't leave any footprints that could give me away.

I waited for the first man to get in position, taking a sadistic pleasure at him being completely oblivious that death shadowed him.

"Alex in position," the man said in a tiny microphone hanging from his Bluetooth earpiece.

"Acknowledged," Stephen's voice responded.

The muffled sound was barely audible, but my enhanced hearing allowed me to overhear his earpiece. As the man sighted in his gun, I slashed my claws across his throat, quickly covering his mouth and nose to prevent his gurgling sounds from reaching his microphone. I disabled my camouflage so that he could stare his death in the face. Wide eyed, shaking with spasms as his life's blood poured out in a heavy flow, he looked at me with disbelieving horror before the light faded from his eyes. Holding on to his jacket with my free hand, I gently lowered him to the ground, satisfied that we'd kept the noise to a strict minimum.

Reactivating my armor's camouflage, I took flight again, gliding down to the vicinity of the second sniper's location. He waited in silence, having visibly already confirmed being in position. As much as I would have liked to repeat the previous kill, the way he stood, leaning against a tree, would have made it too difficult to slash his throat and show my face as he passed from this world. Since getting to Brianna safely without raising the alarm remained my top priority, I bit back my blood thirst and contented myself with snapping his neck.

Once more, I carefully lowered my victim to the ground then stealthily approached the lookout. It could be summed up as a parking lot with a large sidewalk giving a great view of the city, especially all lit up at night. A thick stone parapet prevented visitors from falling to their deaths. Brianna huddled up next to it, her beautiful face drawn with fear as she stared at Stephen and his acolyte, standing near her.

As I closed the distance, I eavesdropped on their conversation.

"Patrick says the medallion still hasn't moved from the church," the man who had attacked me in the catacombs said to Stephen. "So, either he hasn't left yet, or he chose not to bring it."

What? How in Lar's name do they know?

It hadn't crossed my mind that they'd have developed the ability to track the sigil. Good thing to know, and good thing I hadn't brought it with me. They'd have completely bypassed my camouflage.

"The cocky bastard," Stephen mumbled. "If she's right about this mating instinct business, then I'm sure he will come for her."

"But he may have simply said it to butter her up so she would give him what he wanted. For all we know, he was just using her, in which case, he won't give a shit what happens to her," the other man countered.

"Yes, Daniel, there is that possibility," Stephen conceded. "But I doubt it. Even if he's just using her, he didn't put that much effort into seducing her just to ditch her now. He needs her for something, and he'll try to cash in on that investment if possible. And when he does show up, we'll take him out."

Stephen checked his watch.

Twelve minutes remained before 23:00.

"You want him dead?" Daniel asked.

"I don't particularly care, to be honest," Stephen said with a shrug. "London still has one of those monsters captive, and they've already pretty much found out everything there was to learn from it. I just want the damn medallion. Albert has metal piercing rounds," he said, pointing at the man closest to the forest with his chin. "I told him to fire last if things look like they might go belly up. Everyone else has sleeping darts. If the creature has indeed gone into heat over Brianna, it might be interesting to see how that might have affected its anatomy and endocrine system."

"Very well," Daniel said with a nod. "Carl and I have five rounds of sleeping darts each, not counting the snipers. One shot was enough to mess him up, and the second took him out like a light. We should be good."

"Excellent," Stephen said with a malicious grin. "But we still need that sigil. Send a couple of our men to the club to scout out the access to the upper floor. Actually, not men. Send two of our female agents; the sexiest and most ruthless ones we have."

"Acknowledged," Daniel said, getting on his phone.

Anger boiled within me like lava on the verge of erupting. How dare they imply I used Brianna? She'd listened quietly to their conversation, the wounded expression on her face clearly indicating she'd started to believe they might be right.

They know she's awakened my mating instincts. They made her talk.

Another wave of fury washed over me as I imagined the million different, horrible ways in which they could have tortured her. I wanted to lunge at both of them and tear them limb from limb. But that would expose me—and Brianna—to the other two men patrolling the parking area, Albert and Carl. I needed to take out those two before I came back for Stephen and Daniel.

Exiting the tree line, I headed straight for Albert, the man closest to the woods. Sneaking up on him, still hidden by my armor's camouflage, I grabbed him by the waist and threw my victim up in the air, at a slight angle, with all the strength I could muster. He flew up at least ten or twelve meters, giving the illusion that I'd caught him like a bird of prey and was carrying him up to my lair. As I'd hoped, the three remaining agents started firing above him in a pointless effort to shoot me down.

Taking advantage of the panicked ruckus, I charged Carl, located about fifty meters on the opposite side of the parking lot, the sound of my steps covered by the shots. I rammed into him sideways, shoulder first. His arm shattered under the force of the impact, his entire body flying several meters before crashing with a loud thump. Half a second later, Albert's body landed in a tangled mess of broken limbs.

Stephen shouted for the snipers to come in. The resounding silence brought a feral grin to my lips.

"Fuck!" Stephen shouted, realization dawning.

He lunged for Brianna, who had crouched by the railing, hands covering her ears as best as the shackles allowed. Yanking my woman back up on her feet, he aimed his gun at her head.

"Enough of your games, monster!" Stephen shouted. "You're going to go fetch that medallion and bring it back immediately or I'm killing your mate. Don't think I will hesitate."

"Show yourself," Daniel yelled, holding his gun with both hands, eyes wide as he searched for me in vain.

"Yeah, show yourself," Stephen repeated. He lowered his gun and pointed it at Brianna's leg. "You've got three seconds or I'll bust her knee cap."

Brianna sobbed, the tears rolling freely down her cheeks fueling my rage.

"Three... Tw..."

I disabled the camouflage, standing barely five meters from them. Both men yelped at finding me so close. Daniel fired in a panicked reflex. I dodged, lifting my shield in front of me. To my undying relief, it deflected the dart. Well... not quite. The dart seemed to stick into the energy field for a second before falling to the ground. It took me a second to realize the wretched thing had drained a significant portion of the shield's integrity.

Stephen also turned his weapon towards me. I partially turned my skin to stone, the added weight immediately slowing me down. But Daniel fired again. As I feared the darts far more than the bullets, I kept my shield facing him, horrified by the alarming rate at which the darts were depleting it. Stephen's first bullet grazed my upper arm, but the second one found its way into the fleshy part of my left calf, my stone skin preventing it from piercing clean through. I charged Daniel as he fired two more darts.

Only one left before he stops being a threat.

No sooner did the thought cross my mind than my shield collapse. Cold dread coursed through me to find myself exposed on both sides. Daniel's eyes widened, his mouth stretching into a sadistic grin, knowing he had me right where he wanted.

Brianna, who Stephen still held by the upper arm, let herself drop to the ground like a rag-doll, destabilizing him. For a moment, I thought she'd lost consciousness but realized she was actually creating a diversion to give me a chance.

My wonderful mate!

As the stone skin wouldn't protect me from the dart and slowed me down too much, I dropped it and dashed the short distance between Daniel and me. In an effort to keep me away from him, Daniel backed away while readying to fire his last dart. He became tangled in his own feet and fell on his ass. As he scrambled to get back up, I kicked the hand holding the dart gun, breaking a few of his fingers in the process. The gun flew off in the distance, well out of reach. Daniel's pained scream turned into a yelp as I grabbed him by the coat and lifted him off the ground.

"No!" Brianna shouted.

A searing pain in my side nearly made my knees buckle. I dropped Daniel to the ground held on to my rib, where a bullet had dug deep. He scrambled backwards, cradling his wounded hand to his chest.

From the corner of my eye, I saw Stephen taking aim at me again. Although I dodged, I clenched my jaw at the burning sting of the bullet tearing straight through my left wing. Brianna, lying at Stephen's feet kicked the back of his leg, making him fall to a knee, and then kicked the gun out of his hand.

"You bitch!" Stephen yelled, backhanding her.

Her head snapped to the side under the force of the impact, blood pearling at the corner of her lips. I roared with fury and, heedless of my injuries, I ran towards them.

Panicked, seeing his death charging him, Stephen jumped to his feet, yanked Brianna off the ground and, with the strength of despair, threw her over the short railing.

As if in slow motion, I saw the terror in her eyes as she clawed in vain at Stephen's coat. Her scream resonated loudly in my ears. I ignored Stephen scrambling to recover his gun. Heart pounding, I used my momentum and spread my wings. Deviating from my initial target, I flew over his head and down the steep edge, catching Brianna as she plummeted toward the ground.

Straightening out into a glide barely one meter over the mountain's floor, I activated my camouflage and flapped my wings to regain altitude. Stephen fired a couple of shots, one embedded itself in my thigh. I growled in pain but kept flying. Brianna lay limp in my arms, having either lost consciousness from fear, or gone into shock. Each flap of my wings sent a new wave of agony in my side. Taking that piercing round without stone skin had nearly been fatal.

Could still be.

I silently thanked the Rose Syndicate for choosing the Belvedere as the rendezvous point. It represented a short flight to Downtown Montreal, although it felt like an excruciating eternity. My wings felt heavy and my arm muscles burned trying to hang on to Brianna, despite her light weight. Nearly ten minutes after diving over the railing of the lookout, I half-landed, half-collapsed on the roof of The Darkest Hour. Entering my room through one of the many secret entrances I'd built felt like a Herculean effort.

I laid Brianna down on my bed, telling her to remain still. Falling to my knees, I remained still for a moment to regain my bearings while fighting the urge to dive into the peaceful rest of *duramna*. Shaking myself back into action, I quickly checked to see if Brianna had been hurt beyond the slight swelling of her cheek where Stephen had backhanded her. Although she'd regained consciousness halfway through the flight, she still trembled like a leaf.

Satisfied that she was unharmed, I ignored my wounds and fetched her a glass of water. I sat at the edge of the bed and drew her into my embrace. She didn't resist, and accepted the cold drink with trembling hands. She gulped it down, barely taking a second to breathe. Once done, I took it from her hand and put it down on the nightstand next to me.

I closed my wings around her and whispered soothing words in her ears until she calmed down and her trembling receded. The feel of her, safely tucked in my arms, had the most appeasing effect on me. Brianna was meant for me.

"I'm so sorry you got mixed up in this mess," I said, my

voice thick with remorse. "This never should have happened. I should have protected you better."

"There's nothing you could have done," Brianna said with a trembling voice. "They tricked me while I was at work."

She proceeded to tell me what had happened and shamefully explained the interrogation they had subjected her to.

"It's not your fault, my Brianna," I said gently, caressing her hair. "They used some kind of truth serum on you. Very few people could have resisted its compulsion. I'm just relieved they used that instead of any form of actual torture. I never would have forgiven myself if they'd hurt you."

"But what of you?" Brianna asked, leaning back to look at my face and chest. "They shot at you. Are you okay?"

"I'll be all right once I go into *duramna*," I said smiling reassuringly at her.

"Oh my God! You *are* hurt!" she exclaimed, jumping off my lap, forcing my wings open. "Why didn't you say so sooner rather than letting me babble like this? Where?" she asked, pawing at me in search of the wounds. "Where did they hit you?"

She first spotted the slight cut on my arm, then she noticed the blood drying on my side.

"Lift your arm! Where's your first aid kit?" she demanded in a voice that brooked no argument.

"You won't be able to help with this one," I said gently. "It's too deep. A few hours in *duramna* will push the bullet out. But you could help me with the other three bullets I have stuck in me. One is in my calf, the other in my wing, and the last in my thigh. My wounds shouldn't require any actual medical attention. I will just need to rest."

"Four bullets?" she exclaimed, her eyes widening.

I couldn't help the smile stretching my lips at her expression. She couldn't seem to decide whether she was outraged that I'd kept this from her this long, horrified that I'd been hurt this way, or sympathetic at the pain I must be feeling.

My woman was adorable.

"It's nothing serious," I said, rising to my feet and taking off my boots and pants. Sitting back down I swallowed a wince at the pain in my side and lifted my leg on top of the bed to expose my left calf. "You see, when they started to fire, I turned my skin to stone. Most projectiles can't break through it, and my armor provides added protection. It is designed to slow down any piercing object trying to penetrate my skin, and spread out the impact of any blow to reduce chances of fractures."

Extending my claws, I reached for the bullet, only half-buried in my flesh, and carefully extracted it from my leg. Brianna stared in fascination, her eyes flicking from the bullet in my hand to the small hole in my leg, dripping with quickly coagulating blood.

"I will need your help with the other two, though." I said, getting up to fetch a pair of needle nosed pliers from my work desk.

"Doesn't it hurt to walk?" Brianna asked, bewildered, as she shadowed me to my work desk.

I shook my head. "No," I answered honestly. "My leg hurts enough for me to know it has been injured, but not so much as to incapacitate me or make me limp."

I repressed another smile at Brianna's blatant effort at ignoring my exposed cock dangling between my legs. Since I never wore underwear, I had to be quite the sight, naked except for my armor shirt.

"Here you go," I said handing her the pliers.

She took them from my hand then followed me back to the bed. I sat at the edge of the bed then lay down on my side to expose the bullet wound at the back of my thigh.

"Do you see it?" I asked.

"Yes," she whispered, tension clearly audible in her voice.

"Do not fret, Brianna," I said in a soft, reassuring voice. "It barely hurts. Just yank it out. I'd do it myself but it's a little out of reach."

Technically, I could simply go into stone form. During regeneration, my body would naturally expel any foreign substance or object from my body, which could take some time. However, doing it that way would delay the healing process which wouldn't start until the bullet was out—something we couldn't afford right now.

"Okay," Brianna said in a small voice. "Tell me if I hurt you, okay?"

"I promise," I said, knowing that I wouldn't and barely feeling any guilt for the deception.

My female tried to get a proper grip on the bullet, the pliers slipping off a few times. She muttered a curse under her breath, and I repressed another smile. After a few more unsuccessful attempts, Brianna almost managed to pull it out before losing grip again.

"Son of a bitch!" she snapped.

This time, I couldn't help laughing. But the lancing pain from the bullet in my side put a quick stop to it.

"Sorry," she mumbled.

"It's okay, my Brianna," I said, smiling. "These things are tricky. You will get it. There is no rush."

"You know, Alkor, you're the wounded one," she said,

sounding slightly upset. "I should be the one reassuring you that it'll be okay. I'm the most pathetic nurse in the universe. You deserve so much better for saving me."

I frowned at her words. "Nothing can ever be better for me than you. You are not pathetic," I said, looking at her over my shoulder. "You are strong and courageous. What you did back there was extremely brave. You probably saved both of our lives by disarming Stephen. Do not be so critical of yourself or underestimate how amazing you are."

The look she gave me, full of affection and gratitude, melted my insides.

"I wasn't going to let him kill you," she said in a voice where anger, strength, and determination mixed in equal measure. "I didn't just find you only to lose you like that. And you didn't wait all this time to go home only to have a bunch of bigots and fanatics prevent you from doing so. They won't win."

Apparently galvanized by her own words, she clamped down on the bullet with the pliers and yanked it out with one swift movement. I swallowed a hiss at the burning sensation quickly followed by relief as the wound immediately started to close. It would take many hours to completely heal but stone sleep would halve that time.

"Well done," I said, "only one left."

Sitting back up, I spread my wounded wing and Brianna did quick work of removing the bullet embedded there. Once she was done, I pulled her back onto my lap.

She smiled, wrapped her arms around my neck, and rubbed her nose against mine. Her words played in a loop in my head.

"I didn't just find you only to lose you like that."

Did that mean Brianna was seriously contemplating coming with me since she'd also acknowledged that I hadn't waited this long to go home to have those plans thwarted? My tongue burned with the need to ask for confirmation, but I didn't want to unduly pressure her.

"Are you sure you don't want me to try removing that bullet in your side?" she asked.

I nodded. "Yes, I'm sure. It might get pushed further in if we mess with it."

She frowned and nodded slowly, a worried expression on her face. "So, you're going into that stone sleep to heal?" she asked.

"Yes, in a few minutes. But first, I need to warn Lana of what has happened, and that we're both safe."

Brianna nodded again, a serious look on her face. Unable to resist, I leaned in and gently kissed her lips. She smiled, her features softening with a tender expression.

Lar help me, she's stealing my heart.

"I want you to stay here tonight," I said, then cleared my throat, embarrassed that my voice betrayed so blatantly the extent of the emotions she stirred within me. "In fact, is there any chance for you to call in sick for the next few days, or ask for some time off?"

I wanted her to just tell her to quit her job. However, I'd turned her life upside down over the past few days and therefore needed to tread carefully. With luck, I could get her to reach that same conclusion on her own.

Brianna chewed on her bottom lip, pondering. "Time off is not an option, but I could call in tomorrow morning and say I have a stomach flu. That would give me a couple of days and then the weekend will be rolling in."

Four days. Better than nothing but nowhere near enough. I'd ask Lana to get one of her doctor friends to give her an excuse for a longer sick leave.

"Very well," I said. "Let's start with that. But you understand that as long as I am here on Earth, you will not be safe?"

Eyes locked with mine, Brianna swallowed hard and then nodded.

"Now that they know for sure how important you are to me, they will try everything to catch you again. And..." I hesitated to continue.

"And?" she asked, her expression stating clearly she wouldn't let me off the hook.

"And they may still come after you once I'm gone, if only out of spite."

Brianna exhaled loudly, a shiver running through her.

"I told myself I wouldn't pressure you again so soon, but I hope you will seriously consider coming with me," I said in a careful tone. "First because I really want you by my side. The past few days, minus this mess, have been magical. And second, because I will never have a moment's peace, worrying about what might be happening to you. It's a big leap to make, and I'm truly sorry I've dragged you into this, but—"

Brianna covered my mouth with her hand, interrupting me, and then gently traced the shape of my lips with her fingers.

"Standing by that ledge tonight, I thought this time, death would truly get me," Brianna said, cupping my face in her hands. "In the past 24 hours, those men have gone out of their way to try and convince me you'd been using me. That you didn't really care about me, only about what benefits you could draw from me, be it merely sexual gratification, or using me as a tool to achieve your goal. But you don't need me for that."

Brianna shifted on my lap, her fingers roaming over my facial bones, drawing them one by one.

"Dozens of women downstairs would give their left boob for a chance to sleep with you," she said wistfully. "Even blindfolded and shackled so they couldn't see the true you, they'd take it. So, on the sex front, you're covered. And on the devoted helping friend front, Lana also has you covered. You didn't have to come for me. But you did. You could have died tonight, but you took that risk for me. Twice, you have saved my life. No one has ever made me feel more valued and worthy than you have."

"Because you are worthy," I said with all the sincerity that I felt. "You are beyond worthy."

"See? There you go again," she said, her eyes misting. "You make me happy. We've only been together a few days but you've already become a drug for me. I don't want to be without you. Like I said, I just found you and have no intention of losing you. The thought of your world terrifies me, but you're worth taking that chance."

My heart nearly burst in my chest. Tightening my hold around her, I crushed her lips with a kiss that hid nothing of the depth of feeling that was steadily blossoming inside me for her, for my mate, my *Hondassa*.

My hands hungrily roamed over her until a sharp pain in my side tempered my ardor. Although clearly reluctant to, Brianna stopped me.

"You are hurt and need to heal. Call Lana and then go to sleep. Your wounds may not be bleeding anymore, but they're still gaping open. That freaks me out. I wish you'd let me disinfect them or something," Brianna said, glaring at my wounded calf.

I groaned in frustration but acknowledged the wisdom of her words. I reached for my phone and called Lana who answered at the first ring. Realizing that she must have been camping by the device, waiting to hear from me, made me feel guilty that I'd taken this long to tell her all was well. After giving her a quick update, she promised to bring up some food now and fresh clothes for Brianna in the morning.

Putting my regular Durassian pants back on, I stayed up until Lana brought the food. She examined me from head to toe, a worried look in her eyes before hugging me and then hugging Brianna. My chest tightened at the thought of parting from Lana. She'd forever be a mother and a big sister to me. I showed Brianna how the entertainment system worked and, with one last kiss, I climbed onto my perch and entered *duramna*.

10

BRIANNA

Morning found me sprawled in Alkor's bed, all alone. My eyes flicked to his perch where he remained in stone form. Jumping out of bed, I approached his statue and fought the urge to touch him. Since we'd become involved, he'd confessed that he had indeed felt my touch that first time and that it had nearly driven him insane with lust. The playful side of me totally wanted to tease, grab, and stroke. The mere thought of it had me hot and bothered, throbbing in all the right places. I couldn't see any signs of the bullet wounds anymore on his body. The one on his side had closed. Looking around his perch I finally spotted the bullet which had been ejected during the night. As much as I wanted to ask him how he felt, I didn't disturb him, knowing that he still needed to rest, or he would have come out of his stone sleep already.

Still, it fascinated me how his pants had taken on a stone texture similar to his skin. If you didn't know better, you'd never guess that they were clothes, only thinking them some detailing to the statue. With a sigh, I picked up the phone and called my office. They inquired about the emergency that had caused me to run out two days prior. I reassured them that everything was now under control. One of the workers had messed up, but we were able to fix it. I then informed them that I had the runs and would be puking my guts out for the foreseeable future. Thankfully, I hadn't been the type to call in sick often. They didn't question the convenient timing that would effectively give me a four day weekend and just wished me a prompt recovery.

I rummaged through Alkor's closet where I had left a couple of tops and a skirt. I laid out my outfit on the bed then hopped into the shower. I got dressed, deciding to go commando, and hand-washed my undies which I hung to dry in the bathroom. Looking at myself in the mirror, I cringed at the swollen bruise on my cheek where Stephen had back-handed me. Good thing I wasn't going to work after all; it would have been a difficult one to explain.

Finding Alkor still regenerating, I entered the lift and made my way down to the main floor while the restaurant was still closed. A couple of waiters were already busy setting up the lunch service. They nodded at me before resuming their work. I didn't mingle with the staff, not that I would have minded. They always kept a polite distance. I suspected the directive had come from Lana who had thoroughly vetted each employee of the club prior to hiring them. Part of me felt relieved. Like the rest of the patrons, the staff didn't get to come close to Alkor. Knowing I was his girlfriend, they were surely dying to give me the third degree about their boss to get all the juicy details.

I made a beeline for the kitchen and quickly prepared

myself a ham and cheese sandwich, with a side of plain yogurt with honey, and also grabbed a huge Asian pear. If I were going to spend the next four days cooped up inside his apartment, I would have to beg Lana to order a few extra things to bring upstairs so that I could cook for Alkor and myself. I felt like a mooch coming downstairs to raid the restaurant's kitchen.

As soon as I finished wolfing down my breakfast, I cleaned up after myself, and was heading back for the elevator just as Lana arrived.

"Hey sweetie!" she exclaimed, walking briskly towards me, her hands burdened with bags. "How are you feeling?" she asked, a concerned look in her eyes.

"I'm doing great, thank you," I said, smiling back at her.

She was such a lovely lady. There was something entirely maternal about her that fed the gaping hole that my mother's passing had left deep within me. The first time I'd seen her, I'd feared she would be competition. Still in her prime, Lana had a timeless beauty, a refined yet laid back elegance, and an undeniable strength wrapped in silken gloves. Any man would fall for a woman like her. Considering Alkor's venerable age, twenty-eight or fifty years old probably made no difference to him.

"I come bearing gifts," she said, lifting the bags for emphasis.

"Let me help you with those," I offered, extending a hand to relieve her of a couple of them.

"Thank you, love," she said, giving me one grocery bag and one department store bag which I assumed contained clothes.

Efficient as ever, she'd accurately guessed what I needed.

"How is our boy?" she asked as we entered the lift.

"Sleeping to his little stone heart's content."

She smirked, her eyes sparkling with a mischievous glimmer.

"Good, he needs it."

As soon as we entered the room and confirmed Alkor still rested on his perch, Lana helped me unpack and put away the contents of the bags. There was enough food to last two people a week. She insisted that I come down again later to take as many fruits and vegetables as I might need or want.

"I'll be right back," she said before excusing herself.

While waiting for her, I looked through the bag of clothes, grateful for the fresh undies and, overall, impressed with her impeccable taste. The clothes perfectly matched my style, which spoke volumes about her sense of observation. Still, as grateful as I felt, they clearly were quality clothes. She must have paid a pretty penny for them, and I didn't feel comfortable with her spending so much on me, regardless of the delicate situation. I needed to find a way to broach the topic of repaying her without hurting her feelings or offending her.

Lana returned holding two piles of documents in her hands.

"This is Alkor's living will," she said. "And this is yours."

I blinked, my brain tilting for a minute. "Mine?"

She smiled and nodded, gesturing for me to take a seat at the table before sitting down herself.

"Alkor has been busy putting his house in order," Lana calmly explained. "He has tremendous wealth for which he has no need and will be leaving behind. He has been very generous with my family, among others. Although he hopes you will go with him, he has left you enough to guarantee you a life of comfort and luxury for the rest of your days should you decide to stay."

"But… That's insane," I whispered at the impossibly high figure stated on the document, including a couple of estates, and various rare and collectible items. "Why would he do that?"

"He cares deeply for you, Brianna," Lana said with a gentle smile laced with gratitude. "I've never seen him as happy as he has been since he finally let you into his life."

"You set this up, didn't you?" I asked, the sudden realization dawning on me. "You contacted my firm hoping I would come."

"Yes," she said, holding my gaze unflinchingly. "I've watched Alkor pine away for you for the past 10 years, torturing himself over this nonsense of the Prime Directive. I mean, fine, I get that the majority of the population would freak out, but you're his soulmate. He's been head over heels for you since that first time you showed up at the club asking to see him. It was his last chance to be with you. I wasn't going to let him waste it. Alkor is like both a son and a brother to me. I want him to be happy. And I believe you can bring him happiness. You already are."

My throat tightened again, and tears pricked my eyes.

"To think I feared you might be a rival," I said, trying humor to avoid making a spectacle of myself by turning into a weeping wreck.

Lana's eyes bulged, and then she burst out laughing.

"Good God, no. I love him, but stone really isn't my thing," she said with a wink.

I smiled and looked wistfully at Alkor, still sleeping. "Can he hear us?" I asked.

Lana gave him a sideways glance before turning back to me. She shrugged. "Maybe. Sometimes he's only half asleep, so he is aware of his surroundings, like that first time you were... *admiring* the gargoyle statue in the catacombs."

My face heated in embarrassment. Lana chuckled, pleased with herself. I gave her a fake angry glare, which made her laugh even more.

"But I doubt that he is. He's gone deep to fully heal and max out his energy before the journey ahead." Lana covered my hand with hers and gave it a gentle squeeze. "Alkor must leave Montreal as soon as possible and start making his way to the pick-up point. He hasn't told me or anyone else where it is. It is safer for everyone involved. But he cannot stay here any longer, and neither should you. Whatever you decide to do in the end, you should leave Montreal as well."

I swallowed hard and nodded, my mind racing as to how I'd handle my employer. Although I wanted to just hand in my resignation, it would stir too much scrutiny if I did it now. They would promptly assign a new engineer to the project, who would want to come check the current state of the catacombs and get to work—not to mention them asking explanations as to why Lana no longer wanted to work with Stephen's construction firm. We couldn't risk having anyone tampering with the building or the security system Alkor had installed until we were safely gone.

"If you're thinking about your job right now, honestly, you won't need it anymore, even if you choose to stay," Lana said. "Unless of course you love it too much to walk away. But until you've made up your mind, here's a doctor's note dated this upcoming Sunday. It states that you've been diagnosed with a severe *E. coli* infection, which should give you up to ten more days of sick leave. And if you need more time, he will say that complications concerning your kidneys require a longer leave."

"Wow, you think of everything!" I whispered, blown away.

"I'm good at what I do," she said with a smug smile.

I shook my head and laughed.

"I will leave these with you. Although this isn't exactly legal, the Commissioner of Oaths has already signed your living will," Lana said. "If you decide to stay, just burn these documents and come claim your inheritance. If you decide to leave with him, make sure you fill out this form, indicating to whomever you want to donate your wealth, then courier it back to me. I'll take care of the rest."

"Thank you, Lana," I said, genuinely grateful. "I will fill out the document and just leave it here for you."

Understanding my underlying meaning, her eyes widened and then misted. She rose to her feet and cast a motherly look at Alkor before looking back at me.

"I'm so glad you never stopped looking for him," she said. Pulling me in to her embrace, she hugged me, kissed my forehead, then left without another word.

My fingers lingered on my forehead where her lips had touched, like my mother's used to do so many years ago. Settling back down at the table, I proceeded to fill out the forms. Despite being estranged, I donated half of everything to my father, and divided the rest among various organizations that provided assistance to victims of DUIs and to their families. Once done, I picked up a chair and brought it right next to Alkor's perch. Sitting down, I turned on the TV to watch the news, my head resting against his ankle.

I woke up to the rough texture of Alkor's hands caressing my face and my hair, his lips brushing against mine. My eyelids fluttered open to see him looking at me with something akin to reverence. I smiled and clasped my hands behind his neck. He smiled back and picked me up before rising to his feet from his crouching position. I wrapped my legs around his waist while he carried me to bed, eyes locked with mine. He put me down in front of the bed and helped me out of my clothes, his palms and lips roaming over me as he freed me of my shirt and then of my skirt.

It still dangled around my ankles when he pushed me back onto the bed. A satisfied growl rumbled from his chest once he realized I wasn't wearing any underwear, not even a bra. I struggled to kick off the skirt because of Alkor's impatience.

Dropping to his knees before me, he dragged me to the edge of the bed and, opening my legs wide, he dove for my core with voracious hunger. My back arched off the bed when his rough tongue licked my opening in a frenzy before his lips closed over my little nub. A bolt of pleasure and lust exploded in the pit of my stomach, my nipples hardening painfully, aching for his touch. While his tongue teased and massaged my clit, two of his fingers slipped inside me, rubbing my sensitive spot just the right way with every stroke. My stomach quivered, and my legs shook as pleasure quickly built.

I pinched my nipples with one hand while I rubbed Alkor's horns with the other, my nails carefully raking around the bases of the three central ones. He shuddered and emitted that growl of pleasure that always did insane things to me. As if in retaliation for touching his erogenous spots, he intensi-fied the speed of his ministrations until I came apart against his mouth. Even as my body shook with the spasms of release, he continued to lap at me.

Relenting at last, he kissed and nipped his way up over the sensitive skin of my belly before paying attention to my breasts. He particularly loved giving them gentle bites and grazing them with his canines. I had a thing for vampires and both feared and ached for him to give in and sink his fangs into my flesh. Since the first time he had mentioned the mating kiss, Alkor hadn't brought it up again. He didn't want to pressure me as it sounded like a pretty permanent bonding, but I wanted him to.

When he abandoned my breasts, his lips trailing towards my neck, I pushed him back before he could settle down on top of me. As much as I wanted his cock inside me, I wanted him in my mouth first. Before him, I'd never been too crazy about giving head to a guy. It always made my jaw hurt and the choking, gag-reflex part of it, when the guy got overly excited, had never done much for me. But with Alkor… Holy shit! A cock had never tasted so good. I could go down on him for days.

Surprised, Alkor leaned to his side and gave me a ques-tioning look. I pushed him onto his back, pressed my lips to his, and then licked and kissed a trail down his muscular body. I loved the strangely rough texture of his light grey skin. I'd never been with a man with such sharply chiseled muscles and abs. He had the body of a god. But when I edged lower towards my prize, Alkor straightened and yanked me back, making me yelp in surprise. Turning me around, he had me kneeling over his face. I smiled, feeling naughty as I leaned down to take him in my mouth.

It must have been ten years since I'd last done a 69.

My abdominal muscles contracted as Alkor's wicked tongue once more lavished my clit with skillful attention. A moan rose in my throat as pleasure already started building again, deep within. How could I focus on pleasuring him when he so easily brought me to the edge?

Trying to block some of the bliss he gave me, I lowered my gaze to his crotch and wrapped my hand around his alien cock. Long and thick, a slightly darker, bluish shade of grey than the rest of his skin, the rippling ridge along its length would forever keep it from being confused for a human's. He was too big for my fingers to touch but that didn't stop me from giving him a few strokes before leaning down and kissing its head. His shaft jerked in my hand, and his balls contracted, making me smile.

I loved how sensitive he was to my touch and especially to my tongue teasing his head and the small slit at the top. Alkor moaned with pleasure when I tightened my grip as I stroked him, until he rewarded my effort with a bead of semen. I licked it, moaning with delight as the taste of salty caramel exploded on my taste buds. I didn't know if it contained some kind of aphrodisiac or addictive substance, but every time I tasted him, my skin heated, my inner walls contracted with desire, and I ached with the need to have more.

With a hungry moan, I wrapped my mouth around his cock until the head hit the back of my throat. A shudder coursed through him, and he emitted a strangled moan which only fueled my hunger. I sucked him with a feverish energy, reveling in the sensation of his ridges on my lips, his heavenly flavor on my tongue, and his moans in my ears. But even as he neared his climax, my own threatened to rob me of my prize as wave upon wave of pleasure had me riding the edge. Knowing I wouldn't last much longer, I took him as far back in my throat as I could and hummed.

Alkor detonated with a roar, his seed bursting inside my mouth, his fingers sinking almost painfully into the tender flesh of my bum. As I swallowed the sweet and salty treat, Alkor rubbed my clit until I, too, climaxed. The room spun, figuratively and literally, as my lover flipped me onto my back. Destroyed by my two orgasms, I lay boneless on the bed. But he wasn't done with me.

Climbing on top of me, he covered my neck and face with kisses, grazing his canines across my shoulders, before claiming my mouth. His kiss was deep and possessive. He was staking his claim, branding me. Eyes locked with mine, he pushed himself inside of me.

"You are mine, Brianna. Now and forever. No one will ever take you from me."

"Yes," I whispered as he started rocking in and out of me.

I had never felt so full, so utterly possessed as by this man. When I was in his arms, the world ceased to exist. Nothing mattered but him, around me and inside me, his rough skin setting every single one of my nerve endings on edge, his mouth conquering mine, and his body dominating me in every way a woman could want.

"Bite me," I pleaded, needing to be completely claimed.

He froze, the liquid gold of his eyes, darkened by pleasure, seemed to glow. I wiggled beneath him, urging him to continue.

"You want to bond with me?" he asked, hope and uncertainty making his voice quiver.

I nodded, my gaze holding his, unflinching. "Yes. I want to be yours."

"Once I do, there will be no going back, Brianna," he insisted, his eyes sparkling, pleading for me to be sure. "Are you certain you want this?"

"Yes," I said, nodding again. "I've never been more certain of anything," I added with complete honesty.

"My *Hondassa*," he whispered with reverence, making me feel worshipped. "My beautiful mate. Nothing and no one will ever keep us apart."

Something was happening as his throat worked, and his eyes darkened further. He kissed my lips, mouth closed, and resumed pumping in and out of me. After a few moments, his lips parted at last, and the taste of salted caramel invaded my mouth as his tongue tangled with mine. But unlike when I'd gone down on him, this time a strange tingle spread inside my mouth, down my throat, and then throughout my body.

In mere moments, all my senses went into overdrive while a new, hotter, burning lust surged through me. My vision sharpened, my hands and skin felt every subtle detail of his skin, and my ears caught the subtle scraping of his rough flesh rubbing against mine, and even the sound of his claws coming out to play. As if sensing the change in me, and the insatiable hunger taking hold of me, Alkor picked up the pace. Gone was the passionate but gentle lover I'd known from the start.

He snarled, baring his fangs at me, his claws digging into my sides, breaking skin. He'd never looked so alien, so beastly, or so feral. Instead of scaring me, another bolt of lust and need had me moaning his name and writhing beneath him. I felt feverish, my overheating skin somewhat appeased by his cooler temperature as a thin layer of stone covered his flesh. My shout of pain when his fangs sank into my neck was quickly followed by a strangled cry of ecstasy as liquid bliss poured into me through the puncture wounds.

I detonated, my vocal chords all but tearing from crying out so loudly. Relentless, Alkor licked my bite wound then growled his pleasure in my ear as he pounded into me with unbridled fury. Wings spread wide, the molten gold of his eyes glowing, he loomed over me like a demon escaped from the darkest pits of hell to claim his bride. Even his tail whipped savagely at the bedding as if he needed to expel an overwhelming excess of sexual energy. Alkor devoured my lips again, and the same delicious, salted caramel taste added a second wave of tingles throughout my body.

My eyes rolled back when another violent orgasm swept me away. I couldn't say how long he carried on, or how many times he made me fall apart. By the time he finally climaxed, I was drowning in a sea of ecstasy, my voice completely shot from having screamed so much. Seizing me in a bruising hold, his claws digging into my flesh, he roared my name as his seed erupted. Unusually warm as it poured inside of me, the same tingle his kiss had provoked in my mouth manifested itself a hundred times more powerfully in my womb before spreading to the rest of my body, wresting an ultimate orgasm from me.

Completely destroyed, I lay limp on the bed, too wrecked to move. Gathering me in his arms, Alkor rolled onto his back. Holding me tightly to his chest, he closed his wings around me.

"We are one," Alkor whispered, his heart pounding in my ear. "We are bonded for life."

⚜

In the three days that followed, I didn't see any glaring changes, whether to my appearance or otherwise. However, the puncture wounds that Alkor's claws and fangs had inflicted upon me completely healed within hours and so had the bruise from Stephen backhanding me. Alkor profusely apologized for losing control and hurting me.

When I told him I hoped he would claw me like that again, he nearly lost it. I wasn't a masochist and never really contemplated any type of kinky play, but whatever his mating fluids had done to me, his claws hadn't been unpleasant. I mean, yeah, there had been a bit of pain when they pierced through my skin, but it was the good kind of pain. I'd never been so turned on as when he'd gone full gargoyle on me. Errr, rather full Khargal. The partial shift of his skin to stone, rather than irritating my skin as it rubbed against mine, had instead stimulated my nerve endings, enhancing every sensation.

Alkor couldn't swear that no other changes would occur over time, especially the more we continued to mate with him releasing his *dassa*, the mating fluid produced by the glands at the back of his mouth, near his tonsils. Until he'd pointed them out, I'd never really noticed that his speech got slightly slurred from them swelling whenever he would get super horny. Since I'd be leaving Earth, I didn't worry too much about whatever changes might happen to my appearance, as long as they didn't turn Alkor off. I'd love a pair of wings, but would gladly pass on the tail. Alkor said that neither were likely. That didn't stop me from hoping.

But those three days weren't all just fun and kinky play. If not training to build up his stamina, Alkor would fiddle for hours with his gear, especially on a small box to prevent the Rose Syndicate from tracking the sigil, and some other device. After overhearing the conversation between Stephen and Daniel, he realized they were able to track the signal emitted by the sigil, or to track its frequency. We needed to mask it while we traveled so that they couldn't follow our trail. At the same time, we needed a decoy sigil to fool them into thinking it was still sitting pretty in The Darkest Hour.

Thanks to VPN, I connected remotely to my work computer. Sitting on Alkor's couch, cross-legged, my laptop on my lap, I tried to wrap up as much of my work as possible so that my clients wouldn't get screwed over and another engineer could pick-up where I left off without too much difficulty. It saddened me that I wouldn't see some of those projects through, The Darkest Hour ranking at the top of the list.

Lifting my head, I peered at Alkor's beautifully exotic face. His features were set in an expression of deep concentration as he tinkered with a portable version of the solar energy converting device he used to recharge his suit and shield.

"So how do you know how to do all this technical stuff?" I asked. "I thought you were a soldier?"

Alkor raised an eyebrow and looked up at me, his head still bent over his contraption. "Being a soldier doesn't exclude having skills in scientific, technological, or artistic fields. I'm also a pretty damn good cook."

I blinked. "You're saying you're good in all of the above?"

Alkor smiled, straightened and then leaned back against the chair of his work desk. "I'm not too big on science, although my general knowledge probably exceeds that of a majority of the non-scientific and non-medical population. Since I can't just waltz into the doctor's office, over the centuries, I'd kept myself educated in the basics of medicine and biochemistry to try and cater to my own needs. But with our natural enhanced healing and the wonders of *duramna*—not to mention different anatomies—I devoted fairly little time to that.

He looked at all the equipment in front of him and picked up the fake sigil he'd put together to throw off the Syndicate into thinking it was still sitting inside The Darkest Hour long after we'd left with the real thing.

"Now this stuff, I enjoy. I first became tech savvy out of necessity, and now out of passion. It is exciting to try and figure out how I can push primitive technology into performing more advanced functions it hadn't been meant to. This era makes it all the more exciting that humans finally have computers, the internet and nanotechnology."

"So you spent the past thousand years tracking down every bit of tech you could find?" I asked in a teasing tone, but actually wondering how it must have felt to have lived all those eras and witnessed humanity's evolution.

Alkor chuckled.

"Not at all. Decades could go by before any new technological discovery worth looking into popped up," Alkor said with a shrug. "When you have so much time to kill, you learn stuff, whatever is hot at the time. During the Renaissance, I did a lot of drawing and sculpting. During the Age of Sails, I tried to overcome my fear of water, but that didn't work out too well. Plus boats are way too slow when you can fly."

"Fear of water?" I asked, taken aback. "But you saved me from the water."

Alkor nodded slowly, a slight frown on his face as he reminisced. "Yes. But I was flying. Your vehicle had only begun sinking, which is a relatively slow process. Had your car already been submerged, I couldn't have helped you. Khargals can't swim. We're too heavy. I am…" His voice faltered, and he looked slightly distraught. "I am terrified of large bodies of water."

I gaped at him for a moment, the haunted look in his eyes driving home the depth of his phobia.

"And yet, you came for us," I said, even more deeply moved now knowing what fear he had to overcome to rescue us.

"Reflex. It is my duty to protect," Alkor said with a shrug. "But in that specific instance, I think instincts kicked in because it was so reminiscent of the crash when my companions and I were trying to get out of our sinking spaceship. I had to help. I had to save them… to save you."

"I'm glad you did," I said with a smile, allowing both my gratitude and the affection I felt for him to shine through.

"So am I, my Brianna," Alkor said.

The possessive way in which he claimed me gave me a pleasant shiver.

As it turned out, Alkor wasn't just a tech wiz, he also spoke six languages fluently—down from the twenty plus languages and dialects he had learned over the centuries but had now mostly forgotten from lack of use. Where Arabic had proven easy for him in terms of pronunciation, he had given up on Chinese, unable to reproduce the right pitch. Alkor used to play the piano and a plethora of stringed instruments, half of which I didn't even know existed. Finding out he'd had a five-year obsession with playing the harp blew me away. I couldn't quite picture my badass-looking, thick-muscled, sharply-horned Khargal sitting demurely behind a harp.

Through his tales of life over the past millennium, I came to realize Alkor had grown to love Earth and would leave with a great deal of sadness, although I expected most of it would be from parting with Lana.

She would inherit Alkor's network of themed clubs throughout the world. Having managed the operation since the beginning, it only made sense. It warmed my heart that she intended to complete the work in the catacombs. In the two weeks remaining before our departure from Earth, I would work my magic and send her a near final draft of the plans for it.

ALKOR

Too soon, and yet not soon enough, the time of our departure from the club arrived. We would travel light, only carrying the strict minimum—essentially the clothes on our backs and one change of clothes—and plenty of cash as debit or credit cards would be too easy to trace.

The Rose Syndicate had been multiplying their attempts to break into The Darkest Hour. During restaurant hours, 'customers' would get 'lost' on their way to the bathroom, despite them being clearly indicated, and would conveniently find themselves near the lift or climbing the stairs to the upper floors. During club hours, same thing, except some of their agents would try to bribe the staff into leading them to the big boss, or sweet talk VIP members into letting them inside their booths to search for a way into my box located on the same floor. One of them even pretended to be a Hydro-Quebec employee needing to check the counters and electric panels of the building, including every power outlet and heating system to make sure they were up to modern standards. Old constructions were known to be fire hazards, especially now that we operated it as a club.

But one of the senior waiters getting mugged on his way to open the restaurant so that they could steal his access key convinced us the time to leave had come to prevent things from escalating. The rescue mission wouldn't be here for another two weeks. We'd hoped to delay our departure from Montreal for another week so that I could continue to train and for us to be in a safe haven. Despite their various attempts, my private quarters were nearly impossible to break into. With the rendezvous point located in Canada, traveling would be a lot easier as we wouldn't be crossing any borders with all the security headaches that entailed.

After much deliberation, we agreed to travel by train. The rendezvous point was located on Mount Nirvana. We booked a one-way trip to Toronto, and then a connecting ride to Edmonton, Alberta. From there, we'd fly a hydroplane into the Northwest Territories. The whole trip would take five days, including spending a night in Toronto and another in Edmonton.

It would have been faster to take a five-hour private jet flight directly to Tungsten airport. The mostly abandoned mining town sat a stone's throw away from Mount Nirvana. However, you needed prior permission to land there. Even if Lana worked her magic to get us the authorization, we suspected many of the other Khargals would be heading there as well. So many special requests at the same time would raise too many flags, especially considering we would have to wait the remaining two weeks there. A slower transit would keep us moving over a longer period of time rather than sitting still in the same location for too long.

With The Darkest Hour under heavy surveillance by the Syndicate, we needed to sneak out without getting noticed. If we used one of the upper entrances on the roof to fly out in stealth mode, they would suspect we had left by the mere fact that the doorways opened and then closed with no one in sight.

Instead, Lana's sister, Militza, came over to the club with Lana's son, Tommen. I was coming down the stairs just as he was finishing exchanging greetings with Brianna.

"Uncle Alkor!" the boy screamed when he saw me.

Tommen ran and threw himself into my arms. My throat tightened seeing the adoring way in which he embraced me, his small body feeling no bigger than a twig. Smiling affectionately, I caressed Tommen's hair before kissing his forehead. The staff wouldn't arrive for another hour, sparing me from having to wear my perception filter.

"Hello little man," I said. "Did you miss me?"

"Yes!" Tommen said, nodding his head frantically. "Mommy says you have to go back to your planet. Is it true?"

A strange mix of excitement and sorrow laced the boy's voice.

My throat tightened again as I nodded. "My people finally received our message. They are coming to take us home."

"But I was supposed to look after you when I was big!" Tommen said.

"Tommen," Lana said in a disapproving tone.

"It's okay, Lana," I said, smiling at her before looking back at her son. "You're right. And I was looking forward to it, too. You would have been the best protector I could have ever hoped for."

The boy puffed his chest and stared at me with the same adoration that always melted my heart—the same look my younger brother, Marek, used to give me. The longing to see my sibling again warred with the sorrow of parting with this adorable little boy.

"But my family misses me, too," I said softly. "And I miss my home."

"Yeah," Tommen said with a sad face. "I guess I would also miss my family. Will I see you again?"

I let my apologetic expression say it all. Tommen scrunched his little, freckled face and blinked multiple times to keep his tears away. My chest ached as I drew Tommen's head into the crook of my neck and held him tightly, kissing the top of his head. Where Lana had been a mother and a sister to me, her boy had been both a little brother and a son.

Spreading my wings, I flapped them hard, rising a few meters upward. Tommen gasped and lifted his head, looking around him in wonder. I smiled, happy to have chased away some of his sorrow. With a ceiling peak height over thirty meters, I had plenty of room to climb. Once we cleared the side walls, I circled a few times over the VIP booths on the balcony as well as my own private box. Tommen squealed with laughter, the joy in his voice the sweetest music to my ears. With much reluctance, I finally flew back down.

"I'm gonna miss you, Uncle Alkor," Tommen said after we landed. "You won't forget me, right?"

"Never. I have a lot of pictures of you so that I can count all your freckles when I have a hard time falling asleep," I said with a wink.

"Silly!" Tommen said, laughing. "You'll never be able to count them all. You'll get mixed up and then you'll have to start over again. I know. I tried."

We all laughed, and I hugged him one last time, memorizing this instant.

"Thanks for the flight, Uncle Alkor," Tommen said.

"I promised to give you one for your birthday. It just came a little early," I said, ruffling Tommen's mess of red hair.

The boy smiled before going back to his mother.

"You have everything you need?" Lana asked Brianna, falling back into the mother role.

"Yes, Lana, we do," Brianna said with a smile, although I could see emotion starting to get the best of her.

I tapped some instructions into the perception filter on my wrist and then raised my arm so the wrist bracer would face Militza. I held it up for a few seconds. Without having to tell Lana's sister anything, she slowly rotated before stopping once she had completed a full turn. I smiled at her, then approached Brianna. I removed the bracer from my arm and placed it on my woman's, making sure to properly secure it on her wrist.

"All right, love, activate it," I said.

She smiled nervously and tapped on the interface as I had taught her. The air shimmered around Brianna.

"So cool!" Tommen exclaimed, looking at her wide-eyed.

Glancing down at my woman, I smiled smugly to see her clothes now perfectly matched Militza's. A swarm of freckles covered the backs of her hands, her skin the same creamy white as hers.

Yeah, cool, but especially freaky for my woman to now look like Lana's sister.

Brianna walked up to the bar to examine her reflection in the mirrored wall behind the counter. She kept glancing back and forth between her reflection and Militza, a mesmerized expression on her face. Even though I'd been certain it would work, I felt extremely relieved that we'd be able to add new disguise options to the perception filter almost on the fly.

"Looking good," Militza said with a wink.

Brianna chuckled. "Indeed. I'm super-hot."

Militza laughed but then quickly sobered. "Good luck to both of you, and take good care of lumpy head for us," she said, indicating me with a gesture of her head.

"I heard that," I mumbled.

She made a face at me before pulling me into a brotherly hug. Tears pricked my eyes again. I sucked at goodbyes. I wasn't as close to Militza as I to with her sister, but she was part of my adopted human family. She had a good heart and, like Lana, always had my best interest at heart.

Militza released me just as Lana turned her motherly gaze towards Brianna. That seemed to break whatever remained of her resistance. My woman sniffled as a couple of tears trickled their way down her cheeks. Lana pulled Brianna into her arms and held her tightly. She didn't speak, only stroked my woman's hair a few times, and then kissed her cheek. Cupping Brianna's face in her hands, she held her gaze for a moment, letting her eyes speak for her. Lana then caressed Brianna's cheek before letting go of her. The moving tableau made my throat tighten.

Brianna wiped her tears with the back of her hand and then hugged herself as Lana turned toward me. I'd never felt so vulnerable than in that instant. Lana looked incredibly fragile as I wrapped my arms around her. She rose to the tip of her toes to kiss my cheek and then buried her face in the crook of my neck. We held on to each other in silence for a moment. She shivered, and I closed my wings around her, giving her my warmth, my strength, and all the depth of affection that burned in my heart for her. Sorrow clawed at my heart as I kissed the top of her head. I wished she would come with us as well, but she had her own family here and wanted a normal, human life for her son.

After I released her, Lana took a step back and then cupped my face in her hands as she had done with Brianna. She studied my features as if to memorize them, then dropped her arms after one last caress.

"Go on, then. You don't want to miss the train," Lana said, pulling her son to her side for comfort. "Do not take unnecessary risks, but if you have any safe way of letting us know you made it, we'd be grateful."

"Will do," I said, unable to hide some of the trembling in my voice. "Goodbye, and thank you for everything."

With a final nod, I retracted my wings, picked up my gear bag, and then activated the camouflage on my armor.

BRIANNA

After Alkor vanished from view, I accepted from Militza the bag she had brought with her. It contained some clothes, essential toiletries, tons of money, and two smartphones.

I headed out with a heavy heart. Walking out of the club first, I stood outside with Lana holding the door wide open. While we inconspicuously exchanged our last goodbyes, Alkor stealthed out of the building.

"Let's go," he whispered.

Lana didn't hear it, but I heard him loud and clear. Since we'd bonded, my heightened senses had not lessened. The toughest part turned out to be pretending that I was walking on my own towards Place Ville-Marie. I had a vague idea of Alkor's current location and, seeing the throng of people hurrying along the sidewalk on their way to work, I didn't know how he would manage to navigate through them without knocking someone over, or them bumping into him.

Part of me wished he would have flown instead, but with

so many high rises in that area, he would have been forced to fly too high up, not to mention it would make him move too fast compared to me. Nevertheless, Alkor being invisible held another upside. While I casually strolled through the shopping area of Place Ville-Marie on my way to the connecting corridor into Central Station, he looked around for potential enemies tailing me. As soon as we went down the escalator connecting to this new section of the underground city, I stopped at the bakery and bought a small box of pastries, including a chocolate éclair with custard—I was a sucker for those.

As per our plan, we were well in advance, so I lingered a little, browsing the displays of a few shops along the way to the train station. Satisfied that we were not being trailed, I proceeded to buy two tickets to Toronto and made my way to the boarding gate. We still had thirty minutes to kill. I sat on one of the benches, pretending to read on my phone. Technically, I could have, but the words blurred in front of me, my back hurting from too much tension.

"Relax, love. All his well," Alkor texted me from his phone.

I smiled, my heart warming toward my man who had sensed I needed the reassurance.

After what felt like an eternity, the train finally arrived. I boarded, praying that Alkor could follow without too much difficulty. But with all the other people pressing behind me to get on as well, I suspected he would wait until almost everyone was on board to get in.

I made my way to our cabin, my hands still shaking and my heart pounding. Until the train had taken off, and I sat on Alkor's lap, sheltered in the safety of his wings around me, I wouldn't be able to relax. In the meantime, I drew the curtains for privacy from the platform. It seemed time drew on forever before I heard a soft knock on my door. I jumped to my feet and raced to open it. No one stood outside, but a hand gently caressing my breast made me jump back with a small yelp of surprise.

Get out of the way, idiot! How is he going to get in?

Feeling embarrassed for my stupidity, I moved back and felt him brush past me. Casting a quick glance into the hallway to make sure there'd been no witness, I closed and then locked the door to our cabin. I never got a chance to turn around before Alkor's arms wrapped around me, pulling me into his embrace. His hands and mouth were everywhere. There was something insanely exciting and naughty about invisible hands touching me in intimate places.

There wasn't that much space to move around, but that didn't faze Alkor. My clothes flew off me at dizzying speed. The reasonable part of me thought we should wait until the train had taken off, but the impulsive part of me—the dominant one—couldn't wait any longer. Alkor all but dropped me on one of the two padded chairs before drawing me to the edge.

Grabbing my ankles, he placed them over his invisible shoulders. Seconds later the rough wetness of his tongue went to work on my core, lapping at me, sucking my clit, his fingers diving inside of me until he had me chanting his name. Not knowing how soundproof the cabins were, I struggled to keep my voice as low as possible. I wasn't a screamer—well, I didn't use to be—but Alkor had a way of making me explode with serious vocalization. Right before I toppled over the edge, Alkor pulled away from me.

"No!" I cried out, feeling cheated. I'd been so close!

"On your knees," Alkor's disembodied voice growled.

That resonated straight to my pussy, which throbbed with anticipation. I loved when he acted dominant. Impatient, he all but flipped me around when I apparently took too long for his liking. I no sooner got on my knees than I felt his cock press against my opening. Holding on to the backrest for support, I squealed when his hands lifted up my thighs, and he rammed himself home. With my knees no longer touching the couch, I held on for dear life while he pounded into me.

As pleasure washed down over me, I feared my trembling arms would give way, and I'd face plant on the cushion of the chair and end up smothered to death by orgasm—not that I would have cared at the moment. But my grip never faltered, hanging on with a strength I didn't recall ever possessing. With a muffled growl, Alkor released his seed inside me. The slight burning sensation followed by the familiar tingling of his *dassa* sent me over the edge.

But Alkor didn't stop.

Balling me up in his arms, my back to his chest, he held me up and continued to pump in and out of me until we both climaxed again. Turning around, he settled down in the chair, his cock still buried deep inside me. Boneless, sprawled over him, I reveled in his proximity as he disabled his suit's camouflage.

"You will kill me," I whispered, my voice rendered huskier by our little romp.

"Only with pleasure, my *Hondassa*. Only with pleasure."

The trip to Toronto took well over five hours. Alkor used that time to recharge both the camouflage on his suit and the perception filter. In the meantime, I worked a little bit on the plans for The Darkest Hour. So far, things looked good with no signs of us being tailed. After much back and forth, we agreed that I would walk around in my normal appearance—except for a wig conveniently provided by Militza—and he would wear the perception filter.

As I finished packing our stuff, I turned around to find a tall, blond man, with piercing blue eyes, leaning against the door of the cabin, a seductive smile on his lips. He could have been the result of Bratt Pitt and Kevin Costner having a baby.

"Hello, pretty lady. I'm looking for a date. Interested? I shower daily, I eat with my mouth closed, and I put down the seat of the toilet," the man said.

I chuckled and gave him a playful slap on the shoulder. "Stop dicking around, you fool! Grab your bag and let's get going! I want to stretch my legs a little, and we need to find a place to spend the night."

"Yes, Mistress," Alkor said with a mock curtsey.

No one gave us any problems as we disembarked the train and mingled with the crowd hurrying to their different destinations. Ever the gentleman, Alkor carried both our bags as we looked for a motel to hang our hat in for the night. We found a nice one, not too far from the station since we wanted to take the first train out in the morning.

With much reluctance, Alkor agreed to leave our valuables in the room's safe. However, he wore his armor and perception filter, and insisted I bring all of our money in my purse. For his part, he carried the small dampening box containing the sigil in a fanny pack. I couldn't blame him for being overly cautious, but a fanny pack? At least, it was a stylish one made of black leather. With the dark clothes generated by the perception filter, it didn't stand out too much.

We found a nice dim sum place a ten-minute walk from the motel. Thankfully, it wasn't too busy, but just enough to let us know the food would be decent. We settled into a booth in the quietest corner of the restaurant. The dimmed light provided additional privacy and would help hide any potential glitches with Alkor's disguise while he ate.

I ordered far too many variations of dumplings—especially soup dumplings—pot stickers, and fried shrimp balls. Alkor had a thing for the BBQ pork buns. It turned out to be a pleasant evening, the waiters efficient, but non-intrusive.

"Tell me about Duras and your family," I said while showing off my skills with chopsticks as I dipped a potsticker in soy sauce.

It amused Alkor who stuck with the good old fork and knife.

"I have three *khers*, or siblings as you say—one sister and two brothers," Alkor said, his face taking on a faraway look. "Like our parents, we're all of the warrior breed and therefore all joined the army. The Drayvus are part of a long line of warriors."

"Were you all obligated or expected to join the army?" I asked between two mouthfuls.

"No," Alkor said, shaking his head. "We could have chosen a different career path. That would have raised eyebrows, but no one would have given us a hard time about it. It runs in our blood." He smiled fondly as he seemed to reminisce about a specific incident or incidents.

"My parents ran our home with military precision and discipline. That we chose to follow that path was somewhat inevitable."

"But it was a happy childhood, right?" I asked carefully.

It suddenly struck me that I really didn't know much about his world, his people, and how welcome or not I would be in their midst. His broadening smile lessened my rising anxiety.

"It was a very happy childhood. My parents are wonderful. They are strict and swift to discipline, but their love for us is undeniable. My dam is not very good at expressing her feelings. But my sire is quite the funny one. It is common practice for parents to drop their offspring off a cliff when it's time for them to learn how to fly."

My eyes bulged, and I froze mid-chew while waiting for the rest.

"As the firstborn, I was terrified when my turn came. Marek, the second born, was bearing witness to my first flight attempt. He was still too young to fly, but curious as ever, he always shadowed me wherever I went." Alkor smiled fondly thinking of his brother. "I used to call him *bansial,* which would translate loosely as sticky or glue."

I chuckled and resumed chewing as I tried to picture a tiny version of Alkor and an almost twin-looking even smaller version tailing him relentlessly.

"I didn't want him to see me make a spectacle of myself," Alkor said, sobering. "Marek thought of me as his hero. He believed his big brother to be the strongest young Khargal in all of Duras. He swore he'd grow up to be just like me."

Alkor swallowed hard, a wave of emotion overwhelming him. I placed my hand over his and gave it a gentle squeeze.

"You miss him," I said softly.

He flipped his hand around to hold mine and also gave it a squeeze before his thumb caressed my knuckles.

"Yes," he said with a nod. "We were extremely close. My little *bansial*. When I hesitated too long to jump—just eleven seconds after she told me to do so—Mother shoved me off the ledge with the sole of her foot."

I choked on the sip of tea I'd been taking. Putting the cup down, I freed my right hand from his grasp and pressed a napkin to my lips with both hands while coughing my lungs out. Alkor's initially worried look turned to amusement once reassured that I was fine.

"She did what?" I croaked between two coughs.

Alkor chuckled. "She kicked me off the ledge. It is common practice," he added with a shrug at my outraged expression. "But don't worry, she and Father both jumped after me so they could catch me if I seemed in danger of embarrassing myself and failed to fly. Believe me, *Hondassa*, when the ground comes at you at dizzying speed, you spread your wings, and you flap the *grack* out of them."

Although still traumatized by his mother, I burst out laughing. "So you flew?" I asked.

He recoiled, an offended look on his face. "Of course I did," he exclaimed as if the answer had been self-evident.

That made me laugh even more.

"And thus, your heroic big brother reputation remained intact," I said teasingly.

He hesitated, a strange look crossing his features.

"What? Something happened?" I asked, narrowing my eyes at him.

Alkor squirmed uncomfortably on his chair and scrunched his face. How I wished he didn't wear that disguise right now so that I could see the extent of the discomfort on his real features.

"I got a little… cocky as you humans say."

My eyes widened with curiosity.

"Oh, this should be good! Do tell," I said, leaning forward, a smile already stretching my lips in anticipation of his confession.

"I stabilized about halfway down the gorge Mother had pushed me into," Alkor said. "I flew back up which, for my fledgling wing muscles, had been extremely demanding. When I saw *ban*... Marek cheering me from the ground, I got this ridiculous urge to show off. Father told me to land, but since Mother didn't, I kept going, circling around my baby brother while he chanted my name. My exhaustion didn't sneak up on me gradually, I just went from king of the sky to plummeting wreck."

I pressed a hand to my mouth.

"I crashed so hard," Alkor said, wincing at the memory and shaking his head. "Father had to all but scrape me off the ground, while Mother laughed her head off."

"Good Lord!" I said, wondering what kind of mad woman had birthed him.

"Don't judge her too severely," Alkor said with a smile. "Duras is a harsh world. Children need to learn to become tough early on. She knew I wouldn't sustain serious injuries from the fall she also knew would be inevitable. Mother said I was truly my sire's son, typical show off. A few broken limbs would help set me straight. And she was right."

"You broke your limbs often?" I asked, dipping a soup dumpling in the sauce.

"All the time," Alkor said before laughing out loud at

himself. "See, crashing that first day only enhanced my prestige with my brother. Not only had I flown on my own, but I had survived a deadly crash with a mere fracture and a couple of bumps and bruises. Clearly, I was invincible. Godly even."

"Oh God!" I said, shaking my head. "I can't wait to meet him. Your brother sounds like a riot."

"He is," Alkor said, smiling fondly. "You'll like Galtan and Sheira as well. She's the youngest, but she sure loves to bully us."

"My kind of girl," I said.

He chuckled. "I bet."

I sobered and frowned slightly. "But will they be happy to see me?" I asked hesitantly.

Alkor recoiled slightly and stared at me in surprise. "Of course," he said as if that were obvious. "You are my *Hondassa*, my bonded mate. Some of my people live 3000 years and die without ever finding their soulmate. My family will rejoice that *Lar* blessed me by allowing me to find you."

He took both my hands in his and pressed them reassuringly.

"Duras isn't perfect. Water is scarce and that can be challenging for food or certain comforts. Seeing so much greenery —as you have here on Earth—is mind-blowing, a true luxury on my home world. But our people are welcoming of foreigners. Many alien species visit our world, some choosing to settle there, be it for their mate, their profession, or simply because it appeals to them. You will not be rejected for not being Durassian."

"So I keep you happy, and we're all good?" I said, trying to hide my relief behind lame humor.

"That sounds about right," he said, winking at me.

"I can handle that."

"Good. All done?" he asked, pointing at my empty plate with his chin.

"Yes," I said, rubbing my bulging belly while casting a sad glance at the handful of dumplings still sitting in the bamboo steamer.

He waved at the waiter who promptly approached us. After we settled the bill, we left him a generous tip on the table.

"Come, you bottomless pit," Alkor said. Rising to his feet, he took my hand and led me after him out of the restaurant.

Pleased by the nicely cool evening, we strolled along the streets, his arm around my shoulders, mine around his waist, like two lovers without a care in the world. It was, of course, an illusion, but one I fully intended to enjoy while it lasted.

ALKOR

After much debate—we seemed to be doing that a lot lately—Brianna and I agreed to call Militza with one of the smartphones she had provided us to let her and Lana know that things were fine, right before boarding the train to Edmonton. With still no sign of pursuit nor any type of suspiciously lurking individuals, we felt confident that we had fooled our enemies. Despite keeping the call fairly brief, Militza confirmed that the Rose Syndicate had not relented in its efforts to break into the club.

It greatly disturbed me to leave them in this vulnerable position. However, with me now gone, the two sisters intended to file a complaint with the police about random strangers seemingly intent on breaking and entering. They hadn't wanted to call them while I was still in the club to avoid difficult questions or bringing too much scrutiny on me. But now, they hoped to earn heightened police surveillance around The Darkest Hour, making things more challenging for the Syndicate's agents.

As the train raced over the tracks, I devoted a large portion of my time to tweaking my armor and shield, and trying to enhance the perception filter. In the meantime, my mate sat under the domed section of the train, enjoying the view of the landscape while working on the plans for The Darkest Hour. Her determination to see it through baffled me, but it also alleviated part of my guilt for spending so much time training, locked up in our cabin for two—not that she complained.

My beautiful *Hondassa*...

I still couldn't believe we were mated. But as much as it warmed my heart, a part of me wondered if she had truly thought it through, and if she would grow to regret it later. Brianna still suffered from a sense of abandonment by both her parents. Unlike her father, her mother had not chosen to leave her, but in death, she had nonetheless.

In the years since she had reappeared in my life, trying to meet me, I'd spent a bit of time investigating her. She'd closed herself off to most people, never really giving her relationships a fair chance. According to Brianna, most men she'd dated had struck her as not quite honest in their willingness to commit to a serious relationship. I didn't quite believe all those men had truly lacked on that front. Brianna's fear of abandonment had driven her to abandon them first the moment she felt on shaky ground.

It scared me to think she had surrendered so completely to me only because I'd saved her life, thus creating a unique, unbreakable bond between us. I wanted my mate to want me, love me for who I was, not for the sense of safety and stability I could provide. But then, maybe I was reading more into it than I should. Maybe Brianna had fallen as hard for me as I had for her.

If she changed her mind at the last minute, it would crush me.

Terrible thoughts of dragging her on board, kicking and screaming, crossed my mind. Once in space, there would be no turning back for her. However, that wasn't how I wanted to build the foundations of our life together. It wasn't the Khargal way. The thought of taking a female against her will made my skin crawl and my stomach churn. But my heart ached and my innards twisted at the prospect of a life without her.

I could stay on Earth to be with her.

Could I? If it came to that, would I forfeit my one chance to go home and be reunited with my family after a thousand years of waiting? And what of my Warrior's Oath? I had to report for duty. And if the war continued on Duras, I was honor bound to go home and fight for my people. Turning to look out the window of the cabin, my gaze roamed over the breathtaking landscape outside, so many trees, bushes, flowers, and grass. Duras would not offer such lush exteriors. Earth would never replace my home world in my heart, but I couldn't deny having grown to love it over the millennium it had offered me shelter.

Stop torturing yourself and borrowing trouble.

I smiled, hearing myself speak Lana's words to myself. I did have a propensity to worry about things outside of my control or that couldn't be helped. For a blink of a second, I considered underhanded ways of ensuring she wouldn't back out, like letting her know that her long life, accelerated healing, and increased strength would fade, and she would revert back to a normal human without regular doses of my *dassa*. Although it was true, I immediately felt ashamed for having even contemplated that possibility. I wouldn't blackmail her into being my life mate.

If she didn't choose to leave with me, I would resign my military commission and stay on Earth.

But to make sure it didn't come to that, I ended my training and hopped in the shower. In the twelve days remaining before the rescue, I intended to woo her like no female had ever been wooed before.

Remembering some of Lana's tales of romantic evenings with her husband, I squeezed in plenty of 'cuddly times' with my mate—as Brianna always called them. She enjoyed watching movies together, both of us naked, with my wings wrapped around us. Despite the roughness of my palms, my woman loved the daily, full-body massages I gave her. But what she enjoyed the most was cuddling in bed with me while I recounted tales of my youth on Duras. Although she still feared her, Brianna was growing fond of my dam, calling her 'one badass lady.'

She couldn't have been more accurate.

To be fair, my sire was no pushover. As a confident alpha male, he'd never felt threatened by my dam's strength, content to let her assert her authority, which she never tried to impose on him. Mother would love Brianna and adopt her as a second daughter, which I knew would help fill a void in my *Hondassa*'s heart.

Lar willing, she wouldn't change her mind.

We didn't disembark during the couple of stops for people to stretch their legs, in no small part to avoid exposing ourselves to potential prying eyes. Too soon, the train pulled up at the Edmonton station. Feeling confident were weren't tracked and to spare the charges on my suit's camouflage, I wore the perception filter and Brianna remained as herself.

The minute we stepped off the train, I realized our mistake.

I felt his stare before our eyes met. It had been twenty years since I had seen the black hair and washed out grey eyes of that agent, a few weeks after coming out from forty-four years of deep *duramna*. As with every time I came out of hibernation, I attempted to touch base with most of my Khargal brothers. I'd found out that Tas was being held somewhere in London. My efforts to track him down almost got me captured by a relentless fiend called Agent Tulip. For some silly reason, the agents of that division had all taken names of flowers or plants.

But there was nothing pretty or delicate about this specific fiend. What in *Lar's* name was he doing on this side of the ocean, and here of all places?

Tas must have escaped.

Either that, or he was on to another of my brothers who might be coming through Edmonton as well, on the way to the rendezvous point.

I averted my eyes as one would when dismissing a stranger whose gaze they had met. But I remained alert, inconspicuously looking for his backup. He wouldn't have recognized my human disguise. However, Stephen had undoubtedly sent pictures of Brianna to his acolytes. Seeing me by her side, towering over everyone with my 6'7 height, he would naturally draw conclusions as to my real identity.

From the corner of my eye, I saw Tulip walk nonchalantly in the same direction we were heading while calling someone on his phone. Forcing myself to walk at a normal pace, I avoided alerting Brianna while we remained in his line of sight. I could have whispered to her in a tone barely audible to human ears, and she would have heard me loud and clear thanks to the enhancement provided by my *dassa*. Fearing her expression of shock, surprise, or fear might giveaway that we were on to them, I waited until we entered the building.

"Keep a neutral expression," I whispered as soon as we passed the doors. To my relief, Brianna stiffened but her face revealed none of her emotions. "An agent is trailing us. He must have recognized your face. We must find a place for you to put on the filter and for me to go stealth."

With so many people pouring out of the train, many were making a beeline for the bathrooms or the souvenir stores. Leading Brianna by the hand, I headed for a corner of the room where the flow of people provided a living wall. Too focused on their destination, no one paid any attention as I crouched, pretending to tie my shoes. Brianna further hid me from view by standing before me. I activated my armor's camouflage and removed the perception filter bracer before slapping it on my woman's arm.

Getting out of here without bumping into anyone would be difficult, but with the masses already pressing against each other in their eagerness to leave, it shouldn't raise any suspicion. Brianna weaved a path through the crowd with impressive dexterity on her way to the bathroom, but didn't go in. She turned into the corridor on the left and continued instead to a recessed corner with self-service ticket machines, disappearing from view.

I glanced over my shoulder to see Tulip trying to get past the sea of humans keeping him from getting to my woman. He couldn't see her from where he stood, or where she had gone after turning the corner. Looking back in her direction, a grin split my face as I observed a charmingly wrinkled older lady with stretchy, black pants and a red coat with a huge maple leaf—my latest addition to the disguise library—come out from the little nook.

Walking with purpose, Brianna headed towards the exit and the taxi stand. As per our agreement, she would simply hop in a cab and go straight to our intended motel—if she wasn't being followed—or to a mall where we would reconvene. I would follow in stealth flight.

Growing increasingly frantic, Tulip became a bit more brutal shoving his way past the people, earning himself a few tongue lashings, which he ignored. A pretty blonde female, dressed in a black, leather, motorcycling suit walked up to him. He jerked his head towards the bathroom, irritation plain to see on his face. I memorized her face as she rushed into the bathroom, cutting in front of the other women lining up.

Not wanting to linger any more than necessary, I slipped through the swarm, holding both Brianna's bag and mine over my head to avoid them hitting anyone. Thankfully, they weighed next to nothing for me.

As soon as I cleared the automatic doors of the station, I summoned my wings, ran a few steps, and took flight once it was safe to do so. I landed barely two hundred meters later, near the taxi stand where Brianna was queueing for a taxi. Texting her with two bags in hand turned out to be too much of a challenge, but dropping them to the ground would make them visible. Closing the distance between us, I brushed against her arm. She stiffened slightly in surprise.

"Safe," I whispered in that almost inaudible tone.

A discrete smile blossomed on her lips, confirming she

had heard me. I stood nearby, out of people's way, until she got into her taxi and on her way to the motel. One last look at the station revealed the pair of Rose Syndicate agents fuming at the entrance, their heads jerking this way and that, looking for us in vain.

Resisting the urge to go eliminate the threat, I took flight again and followed the vehicle carrying my mate to safety.

⊱✿⊰

"From now on, you must keep using the perception filter while we travel," I said to Brianna, as I spooned her on the motel bed.

"But it will drain too fast, same as your armor," she argued.

I smiled and nuzzled her neck.

"They will last longer than you imagine," I said gently. "I'm just overly cautious when it comes to using them. But it can run for a few hours. I have a portable charger so that you can replenish it during your flight to Virginia Falls. It's not as effective, but it should help prevent a disaster."

"*My* flight?" she asked, looking at me over her shoulder with a shocked expression.

"Yes," I said, nodding. "I will fly alongside the plane. It is safer that we're not seen together. My height makes me stand out too much," I added quickly when she opened her mouth to argue. "Now that the Rose Syndicate is alerted to our presence in Edmonton, they will be surveilling every train station, bus stop, and airport. They know your face and a wig can only get you so far. Even if you wore a burka, if they see a man my height with a female your height, they will know right away."

Brianna turned around to face me, a worried look on her face. "You're going to be exhausted."

I laughed. "No, my love. I can fly for hours over a very long distance without tiring. Carrying someone else is a bit more challenging, but you're so light, I barely feel it. The real killer is flying with stone skin. It weighs me down a lot and slows my movements. That drains me in no time. That's why I had been so keen on training lately. All will be well." I brushed her hair from her face, and caressed her lips with my knuckles. "Is there any way you can speak with a deeper, more manly voice?"

"You want me to wear a man's disguise?" Brianna asked, surprised.

I nodded. "It will draw far less attention to you. The agents will be looking for a female of your approximate height. They are aware of the perception filter but haven't managed to see through it… yet. If you stroll in as a man in his early twenties or his late sixties, they are less likely to pay you much attention."

"Hmm, good point," Brianna said with a slight frown. "How do I sound? Is that manly enough?"

The sting of my fangs sinking in my tongue kept me from bursting out laughing. No one in a thousand years would ever believe her to be a male, even pretending it was one that had been castrated before reaching puberty.

"That was a valiant effort," I said cautiously, fearing a bout of laughter the instant I began talking.

"That means I suck," Brianna said with the loveliest pout, her shoulders drooping.

"No, you don't," I said, giving her pouty, bottom lip a little nip. "But when you do, you do so magnificently."

She blinked, not understanding at first and then gasped, looking both shocked and amused as she gave me a friendly slap on the upper arm.

"You perv!" she mumbled.

"Hardly. I'm merely giving credit where it's due," I said teasingly, though kicking myself for this reminder of how my mate's mouth around my cock always brought me to the brink of insanity. One day, she'd kill me with pleasure.

"Be that as it may," Brianna muttered with an adorable blush reddening her cheeks, "that doesn't change the fact that my male voice is pathetic."

"You're too hard on yourself, *Hondassa*," I said, caressing her throat with the back of my hand. "It's not pathetic. But you are the embodiment of femininity in all its grace, elegance, and strength. It would make no sense for you to have a manly voice."

"You evil flatterer," she said, failing miserably to sound stern. "I don't deserve you."

The emotion in her voice made my heart ache with the strength of the feelings blossoming inside me for my female.

"I don't deserve you," she whispered again before kissing me.

I responded in kind, our tongues mingling. It was filled with affection, tenderness, and something special I couldn't describe, devoid of any of the lust that had been rearing its head moments ago.

"You more than deserve me, my mate," I whispered against her lips. "I've waited centuries to find you. I thank *Lar* every day for bringing you to me and giving us the chance to be together, against all odds."

Brianna's mouth worked as she seemed to hesitate to

speak the words that clearly burned on her tongue. I didn't need to hear them. I didn't want to hear them until she was ready and certain. My woman's eyes told me all that I needed to know.

"Sleep, my *Hondassa*. Tomorrow, we go buy the tools needed to make you a voice modulator."

Her eyes widened. "You can make one?"

"Of course," I said with false outrage. "I'm an alien with advanced knowledge. I can do anything!"

She giggled and gave me another friendly tap. "Silly man."

"Only for you, Brianna. Only for you."

She smiled and cuddled against me. I held her until she fell into a deep sleep, then snuck out of bed. Being a creature of habit, I yearned for my perch but settled on the floor before entering *duramna*. I didn't truly need it, but I preferred to be overly cautious by keeping myself fully rested and healed at all times.

The next morning, Brianna's dainty fingers teasing my nipples pulled me out of my slumber. I had been aware of her waking but remained in this hazy place between the dream world and wakefulness. I tried to remain stoic under her touch, but my cock once again betrayed me. Coming out of *duramna*, I tossed her on the bed and showed her what happened when an irresistible female awakened a sleeping Khargal—not that she complained.

We ate a quick breakfast at the motel's dining room, then agreed that I would head out on my own to acquire the parts I needed for her voice modulator. Brianna would remain locked up in our room and wouldn't open to anyone. If only we'd been on Duras, I'd simply have made her drink some juice of *tamsiak* that would have made her sound like a male for a few hours.

She used the pretext of going to fetch some ice from the ice machine, allowing me to leave the room in stealth mode. It took a little longer at the entrance for someone to finally exit so that I could shadow them. Before leaving, I made a reconnaissance flight over the perimeter of the motel to make sure no suspicious vehicle or individual had the place staked out.

Although reassured when I could not detect anyone, I remained stressed the entire ninety minutes it took me to fly to the closest electronics store, find the parts or items I could extract from them, buy a new travel bag for Brianna and return to the motel.

It took all my willpower, upon re-entering our room, not to draw my mate in to a bruising hold. I couldn't let her know how much I'd worried. She relied on my strength and confidence to get through this ordeal. Seeing me this frazzled would undermine her faith in me and not help her already challenged peace of mind.

It took me an entire day to assemble the voice modulator. It wasn't the spectacular success I had hoped for. I could only go so far with the pieces I had. Although it did modify her voice, she had to speak in a bit of a hush for it to work reasonably well, making her sound like someone who had abused alcohol and cigarettes.

We spent the following day making her practice using it, walking, and acting like a man. The hardest part for her was to not sit ladylike, knees together, feet slightly to the side. I kept reminding her to pretend she had a grapefruit lodged in her crotch. That made her laugh until I actually did stuff her crotch with a carrot shaped plushy to give the impression she had a cock.

Brianna wasn't amused.

The delay turned out to be beneficial. While my mate trained her manly skills, I made additional tweaks to my armor to increase the flight time in stealth mode. But those couple of days also made our trail grow cold. The agents who had been camping out at the main transportation venues would be thinking we'd long ago moved on.

Or so I hoped.

14

BRIANNA

I paced back and forth, trying to work up the courage to call my father. Once we left the motel, we'd pretty much leave civilization. There were no guarantees that the phones Militza had provided would still work once we reached the cabin we'd stay in for the seven days remaining before the rescue ship arrived.

Alkor had offered to grant me some privacy while I talked to my dad, but I asked him to stay. A part of me needed his strength near me. The other part of me feared he would be disappointed to see me fall apart and turn into a complete emotional wreck.

Three times already, I'd dialed the number and hung up instead of pressing the call button. I wasn't a child. Not anymore. I could do this. I needed to do this. Taking a deep breath, my eyes connected with Alkor's. He smiled encouragingly and nodded. I swallowed hard, dialed the number, and tapped the call button with trembling fingers. My stomach knotted a bit more with each ring, both dreading and hoping he wouldn't pick up.

On the fourth one, he did.

"Hello?" my father's voice answered, his curiosity at not recognizing the number plain to hear.

Since Mom's death, Father's circle of friends had considerably shrunk as he increasingly isolated himself. Once he'd met Merryl, she became the center of his universe, and her also limited circle of friends became his.

"Hello, Dad," I said, pleasantly surprised by how stable my voice sounded.

"Pumpkin!" Dad exclaimed, visibly stunned. "I didn't recognize the number. What's wrong?"

I instantly felt a wave of bitterness wash over me.

"Does something have to be wrong for a daughter to call her father?" I said with a slightly harsher tone than I'd intended.

"No, of course not," he replied on the defensive. "It's just unusual for you to call on a whim. I worried is all. So… How are you?"

I bit my bottom lip. This isn't how I had planned on starting this conversation.

"I'm doing good. Really good," I said in the gentlest voice I could summon. "I… There's a lot happening in my life right now. Some wonderful things."

"Oh?" my father said, although it sounded more polite than really interested.

"As you may remember, I met someone."

"Yes, yes. That's very good," he said, with the same distracted tone.

"That's very good," I echoed, the bitterness seeping back

into my voice. "You know, most fathers would already be giving me the third degree. What's his name? What does he do for a living? What's his religion? Who are his parents? What do they do? Where does he live? Where did you meet him? You know, the stuff fathers worry about when they give a shit about their daughter."

"Hey, young lady! Watch your language! I raised you better than that!" my father exclaimed.

Something inside me snapped.

"No, Dad, you didn't raise me better than that. In fact, you didn't raise me at all because you were too fucking busy punishing me for looking too much like Mom!" I shouted. "I lost her, too! I lost both of you that day. You might as well have died, too, for all the difference it made!"

I slapped my hand over my mouth, shocked by the venomous—but true—words that poured from my mouth. A heavy silence answered me, the sound of my own breathing roaring in my ears. Heart pounding, I waited for my father to say something, anything, even if to yell at me.

"I'm sorry. I shouldn't have said that," I stuttered when the silence stretched. "Dad? Dad? Please say something? I didn't mean it."

"Yes, you did," he finally answered with a tired voice. "And you're right. I couldn't stand looking at you. It hurt too much. I still can't."

My heart all but shattered inside my chest and tears burst from my eyes. Without a word, Alkor came to stand behind me and wrapped his arms around my waist. Trembling, I leaned back against his strong chest, needing every ounce of his strength.

"I failed you as a father, Brianna," my father said, his

voice shaking with repressed tears, "but it was never your fault. It was always mine. Your mother was everything to me. It's been twenty years, yet it still hurts as much as that day. Sarah had always been the strong one, and so are you."

My throat constricted to the point where I could barely draw in any air. In all these years, my father had only ever shown me a politely cold and distant front, never this deeply emotional, wounded, broken man.

"I never wanted to hurt you, Brianna. You are and will always be my little pumpkin. I do love you. I'll always love you. But I hurt you more by being around than away from you. Not because of anything you did, but because I am weak." My father drew in a shuddering breath when he heard me sniffle through the phone. "Don't cry, pumpkin. Please don't cry. I didn't ask you about your boyfriend because it shames me to have failed you, because I think of you walking down the aisle and how you would look angelic, exactly like Sarah had and… and…"

Hearing Dad weep over the phone broke me. In all those years, resenting him for abandoning me, I had never realized how utterly Mom's death had devastated my father, even to this day. I had spent so much time resenting Merryl for stealing his affection from me, and for trying so hard to erase his memory of Mom. Now, I actually felt sorry for her. How horrible it must be to be married to someone you love —and I never doubted Merryl's love for my father— knowing that his heart would always belong to another now beyond the grave.

"I forgive you, Dad," I said, wiping my tears with the back of my hand. "You did what you could, and I didn't turn out too bad. So you did something right." I said with a teary laugh. "I love you, Dad. And I… I'm glad we've finally talked about this. I thought you hated me."

"Oh Bri… Never! Never, sweetheart!" my father exclaimed. "You're my baby girl."

"Your all-grown-up baby girl," I said, smiling through my tears. "Dad… I'm going away for a really long time," I said, sobering. "This is probably the last time we'll talk."

"What's going on, Bri? Are you in trouble?" Father asked, worry replacing his sadness. "Is it that guy? He's not in some kind of cult, is he?"

I burst out laughing. "No, Dad. Alkor is definitely not in a cult. And if he were, I doubt he would have let me call you to give you a heads up."

"But he's the one taking you away, isn't he?" Dad persisted.

As much as his prying worried me, it soothed a painful ache deep in my soul. I'd heard him say he loved me, and I believed him. But in this instance, I felt his care; I had my father back.

"Yes. He asked, and left the choice up to me. I have *chosen* to go with him. Nothing ties me here, and he's amazing to me."

"Let me talk to him," Alkor whispered in my ears.

I hesitated for a second before nodding. "He wants to talk to you," I said hurriedly to my father and passed the phone to Alkor without waiting for his response.

I pulled out of his embrace and turned around to face him. Eyes locked on his serious face, I bit my bottom lip and twisted my hands with anxiety. Alkor put the phone on speaker.

So much for wanting Dad to meddle in my affairs.

"Hello Mr. Brent," Alkor said, his voice suddenly more gravelly, like when he turned to partial stone form. "My name is Alkor Drayvus, your daughter's mate."

Silence met his words. My stomach knotted, my anxiety skyrocketing. I cast a worried look at Alkor who smiled at me reassuringly.

"I know that voice..." my father finally whispered, sounding halfway between awe and fear.

"You do," Alkor acknowledged stoically.

Baffled, I raised a questioning eyebrow at him. He caressed my cheek but didn't comment otherwise.

"It... It was you... That night, it was you," my father said.

"Yes."

My father insisted. "With the golden eyes and the... the..."

"Yes," Alkor repeated again.

While Dad exhaled a shuddering breath through the phone, my blood suddenly turned to ice.

He knew! Oh God, all these years, he knew I hadn't hallucinated the gargoyle!

"You've come back for her... for my baby girl, haven't you?"

"I never left," Alkor said in the same neutral voice. "However, it is now time for me to return home to my people. But no place will ever be home without Brianna by my side."

My throat tightened, and I pressed myself against him. He wrapped his arm around my shoulder and gently kissed my forehead.

I didn't know what to think anymore, or how to feel. In the months that had followed the crash, Father had done everything to convince me I'd imagined the winged creature that had saved us. He'd insisted that demons didn't save people, they killed them. If I kept telling crazy stories, the doctors would put me in the crazy house with all the other crazies. He'd been correct, of course. Had he told the cops a demon-looking creature had dragged us out of the wreckage, he would have ended up in the loony bin with me right beside him.

"Is… Is that payment for…?"

"NO!" I exclaimed. "No, Dad. Alkor gave me a choice. I am going with him of my own free will. He makes me happier than I've ever been."

"Brianna's happiness is paramount to me," Alkor said gently. "Taking her by force would defeat that purpose. Not to mention that my people would execute me for committing such a terrible crime."

My father exhaled noisily again. My heart ached for him, for us. Despite the distance between us, seeing him again had always been a short flight away. There would be no more opportunities going forward.

"You… you will protect her, like you did that day, right? You'll keep my baby safe?"

"With my life. Now and always," Alkor pledged. "This, I, Alkor Drayvus, swear to you, Mr. Brent."

"When... When are you leaving?" Father asked, his voice defeated.

"As soon as we hang up, we will head for the rendezvous point where his people will pick us up," I said, remaining vague for all of our sakes.

"I love you, pumpkin. I'm sorry…"

"Don't be. You made me the strong woman I am today. I love you, too, Dad. Promise me you'll be happy."

"Only if you promise me the same."

"I promise," I said with a teary giggle.

"Farewell, Mr. Brent," Alkor said.

"Farewell, son," Father said. "Thank you for saving my girl. For saving us."

"It has been my honor," Alkor replied.

"Goodbye, pumpkin. Spare your old man a thought from time to time."

"I will. Love you, Dad."

"Love you."

❦

With seven days left before the rescue's arrival, we left the motel in a one-way rental car. The tinted window allowed us to complete the seven-and-a-half-hour drive to Footner Lake in our normal appearance, thus avoiding wasting energy on both Alkor's suit and the perception filter. Only once we approached the gas station in High Level, a short distance from the Footner Lake High Level Airport, did he turn on his armor's camouflage while I activated my male disguise. I stopped to fill the tank, and opened the passenger door to let Alkor stealth out before pretending to clean a mess on the dashboard.

Although I couldn't see him, he flew alongside the vehicle until I reached my destination.

"Hello, my name is Mr. Peters. I have a reservation," I said out loud, testing my male voice one last time in the car.

My stomach fluttering with stress, I carefully pawed at the voice modulator plastered on my throat. A black turtleneck sweater hid it in case I needed to deactivate my disguise.

Taking in a deep breath, I picked up my black, leather, travel bag which Alkor had bought in town, and stepped out of the car. I walked up to the National Car Rental service counter and handed over the keys for their inspection. To my relief, the clerk didn't seem to find anything off about me.

I entered the airport's terminal, paid the fare, and was driven to the lake a short distance away where my hydroplane awaited me. I hated not having Alkor by my side, but this time, having a free hand, he texted me that all was well while I waited to board the plane.

Already feeling tired after that long drive, I feared falling asleep during the less than two hour flight to Virginia Falls Waterdrome in the Northwest Territories. Thankfully, the breathtaking view of the untamed Canadian wilderness kept me wide-eyed. The pilot, a charming man in his late forties, also played tour guide during the flight. As we landed, I kicked myself for all the wonders of my own country I'd never taken the time to discover, too busy being… busy.

And now I would never have the chance to see them again.

After an uneventful flight, I got off the plane, famished, itching for a shower, and a warm bed to cuddle in next to my man. But we weren't there yet. To my relief, Mr. Murdock, the owner of the cabin we had reserved in the Nahanni National Park, was already there, waiting near the water-drome, despite our slightly early arrival. He gave me a ride to the cabin located barely thirty minutes away by car.

This area was unbelievable. Under different circum-stances, I would have loved to spend some time hiking and camping here with Alkor. Mr. Murdock gave me a quick tour of the three bedroom cabin, its large wooden patio in the front overlooking the lake with an incredible view of the great outdoors.

Naturally, he wondered at me being up here by myself in this big place, with no means of transportation. I pretended to be a writer in desperate need of isolation to finish a novel I'd been struggling with by the end of the month. As per my request, he'd filled the fridge and cupboards with enough food to last me a little over a week. We agreed he would return on the first of November for a tour of the premises and to take me back to the waterdrome. Despite his kindness, I couldn't have been more relieved when he finally left.

No sooner had his car started driving away than Alkor's arms closed around me, and his camouflage deactivated.

"We did it," I whispered.

"We did it," he repeated, nuzzling my neck.

"Did you see anyone?" I asked.

"No. Nobody trailed us, and I found no agents lurking nearby. I will keep checking every day, but for now, we appear to be in the clear."

"From your lips to God's ears," I said, turning around in his embrace. "Seven days. Seven days and it will finally be over."

"Seven days and I will take you to your new home," Alkor said before capturing my lips.

❧ 15 ❧

ALKOR

I watched Brianna taking a dip in the lake, my stomach twisting with anxiety. Khargals didn't do well in the water; we sank like rocks. As she glided effortlessly through the water, images long buried in my memory came back to the surface. My crewmates bruised, battered, and those severely injured by the crash, fighting against the violent current attempting to drag us to our deaths. So many wasted lives.

Five days had gone by since our arrival. Five days of peace. Five days of anxious waiting. My instincts had been growing increasingly unsettled, the sense of impending doom weighing heavily on me.

The calm before the storm.

However, I'd been saying that since our arrival, and nothing had happened. Maybe I was overthinking things, as always. And yet…

I didn't hide my relief when only a few seconds after going in—although they felt like forever—Brianna climbed

182

out of the lake, like a water nymph. She strutted towards me, her dark hair plastered to her shoulders. I rushed to her with a towel, hating that she'd gone into such cold water, even for a second. But she had this thing about how Finnish people would go from the sauna into the cold, then back into the sauna. We didn't have one of those here, just a hot tub on the far side of the patio from which she had just stepped out moments ago.

Brianna gladly accepted the towel and smacked my behind before running back to the Jacuzzi. With the sun already setting on the horizon, I felt a little less worried about walking around without my disguise on, especially considering I'd done another perimeter patrol only moments prior. It still worried me that we were a relatively short driving distance from the waterdrome. But at least, any car driving up here would be easy to detect.

I helped my female into the hot tub before joining her. Any doubt that my *dassa* had enhanced Brianna had vanished since our arrival in the Northwest Territories. Despite growing up in Montreal where winters could be fairly harsh, my woman had never been too keen on the cold, wearing layers upon layers of clothes at the first signs of a brisk wind. But now, like me, the cold barely seemed to bother her. That dip in the river should have had her turning blue within seconds, but the frozen water had barely nipped at her.

Still, it had been enough for her nipples to harden, and her perky breasts to tighten. As I sat next to her in the Jacuzzi, my tail wrapped around her knee, spreading her leg wider before trailing a path up her inner thigh. Brianna's lips parted. I chuckled at the way she eyed my tail warily.

Up until now, I'd never brought it into play. But our

conversation with her father, and the past five days together in what could have been deemed a lovers' retreat, had built my confidence that she truly cared for me and wanted me with all my differences. Gratitude and hero worship didn't drive her desire to be with me.

Still, my shoulders tensed as I spied her reaction while my tail wormed its way to the seam of her pussy, the rounded tip caressing her slit in a slow up and down motion. She inhaled a sharp breath, the muscles of her stomach contracting. Her blue eyes darkened as I accelerated the motion of my tail, and my right palm closed around the perky globe of her left breast. Drawing her face to mine with my free hand on her nape, I captured her lips in a passionate kiss. She moaned, her legs parting wider to grant me greater access.

Gladly accepting the underlying invitation, I pushed the tip of my tail inside her. Although of a smaller girth than my cock, I penetrated Brianna carefully to avoid hurting her. She gasped, and I swallowed her next moan only to utter one of my own when her dainty fingers wrapped around my shaft. Breaking the kiss, my lips trailed along her jawline to that delectable little earlobe, which I greedily sucked on. I accelerated the movement of my tail inside my woman, trying to ignore the fire in my groin growing with each stroke of her hand on my cock.

Letting go of her breast, I reached between her legs, my fingers rubbing her engorged clitoris. She cried out, her back arching against the side of the Jacuzzi. My mating glands swelled, and I didn't hold back, gladly welcoming the burning flow of my *dassa* spreading through me.

My fangs ached with the need to inject my female with my essence. Biting wasn't necessary to bond our mates. My *dassa* mingled with all my body fluids. But the urge to bite had been a hereditary trait in my family and not an uncommon one with many other bloodlines. And now, as my mate neared the edge, I sank my fangs into the tender flesh of her shoulder, injecting her with my *dassa* in its purest form, sending her tumbling over in a whirlwind of ecstasy. Even as she cried out my name, her body shaking with spasms of pleasure, I reveled in the blissful pleasure of the bite.

As Brianna started to come down from her high, I pulled out my tail and, drawing my woman onto my lap, I impaled her on my cock. Clenching my teeth at the exquisite tightness of her sheath squeezing me from all sides, I pressed her slender body to mine, caressing her soft skin while she adjusted to my girth. Our lips met again, and she shuddered as the tingling heat of my *dassa* invaded her mouth. I intended to renew that bond often, to strengthen her and extend my mate's life to match the 1600 years that still remained to my own lifespan.

I started pumping in and out of her, hissing with pleasure as my mate clawed my back and nipped at my chest and shoulders. Each of her gentle bites sent bolts of lust straight to my groin. Brianna had begun doing that since we'd bonded. I didn't think she realized it, no doubt acting on an instinct she'd inherited from me. I wanted her to sink her teeth harder, which she'd subconsciously started doing as well. Her nails had hardened, giving me a most delicious burn every time she raked them alongside my spine. In time, I believed she'd develop retractable claws like mine.

Water bubbled and splashed around us as I increased the pace. Her burning skin rubbing against mine also hardened ever so slightly, enhancing the sensation on each of my nerve endings. Brianna would never fully develop stone skin like mine, but I could already see she'd achieve partial levels for both defensive and pleasurable purposes. A few more pumps later, my mate fell apart, swept away by another orgasm. My release crashed over me as her inner walls clamped down on my cock. My seed erupted, the searing bliss of my *dassa* pouring out into my woman, enhancing her climax, and bonding with her DNA. Soon, Brianna would be completely compatible with me.

And, Lar willing, soon my seed would take root.

My eyes snapped open seconds before the proximity alarm of my perimeter surveillance system went off. The sense of impending doom had stirred me out of my *duramna*. Shifting out of stone form, I reached for Brianna, still deeply asleep in the bed next to me. She startled awake, and I gestured for her to be quiet and to get dressed. Eyes widened with fear, she nodded and swiftly got out of bed. Despite my worry, I smiled internally, watching her move around the room quietly and efficiently, not realizing she hadn't turned on the light; my mate no longer needed it.

Having taken the habit of sleeping in full armor, I shoved my feet into my boots, a gift from Lana who had them specially made to replicate my former ones, which had fallen to pieces after decades of use. While Khargal feet didn't look radically different from a human's, normal shoes didn't really fit our greater width.

I fetched my tablet linked to the motion detectors, which

I'd configured to ignore the occasional wildlife that lurked in the vicinity of the cabin. A quick look at my screen showed five intruders. They'd believed themselves cunning by sneaking up from the woods behind the house rather than coming up the road.

"Stay inside," I whispered to Brianna in that sub-human hearing voice, more grateful than ever that she could perceive it. Although the men were still one hundred meters away from the house, they could have some long-range listening device.

"Alkor, don't go out!" she pleaded.

"It is better I take out the ones that are isolated rather than have to deal with all five together," I said in a pressing tone, eager to get to them before they got to us. "They will have weapons and possibly those sleeping darts again. If they get me, we're both done for." I kissed her, silencing the arguments rising on her lips. "I promise to return," I said before going into stealth mode and making a swift exit through the patio door.

Closing the door behind me, I turned the outer layers of my skin to stone, both as extra protection against projectiles, but also to make myself invisible to infrared in case they used it. The extra weight immediately affected my dexterity and speed. Flying around the side of the house and into the woods, my enhanced vision allowed me to zero in on one of the two, somewhat isolated men. Among the five, I recognized Stephen and Daniel with a third man I didn't know. The other two men flanking the sides were also unfamiliar to me.

Like a bird of prey, I swooped down on the man on the left, snapping his neck in a fly-by. He collapsed to the ground, dead, never realizing what had befallen him. Gliding around to the opposite side, I intended to repeat the same tactic with the other isolated man, but some kind of bird, also swooping down straight in my path, bumped against my wing. Its panicked cry drew the attention of my intended prey who saw the bird tumbling over the invisible platform of my spread wings. On instinct, the human ducked, moments before my hands could reach for him. Frustrated, I shed my stone skin for speed, then flew a short distance before circling back. Still a bit stunned, the bird recovered and flew off just as my target started running towards his companions, raising the alarm.

Flapping my wings with a vengeance, I dipped down and spread them wide. Adjusting to his height, I flew past him, the sharp edge at the top of my wing neatly beheading him. With an enraged cry at the sight of their fallen comrade, Stephen and Daniel dashed towards the cabin while their remaining acolyte fired darts at me. I rolled out of its path, raising my wrist in front of me, the rectangular energy shield forming just in time to block the next ones he shot in a continuous barrage, dart guns in both hands. My shield flickered, the darts' devastating effects against it quickly unraveling it.

Still flying, I shot towards him, smashing the weapons out of his hands with my shield. Without slowing down, I snagged him by the back of his shirt. Despite the pain he no doubt felt in his hand—that could be broken for all I knew considering the strength of the blow—he tried to hang on to my forearm, screaming as I gained height and circled back around the cabin. My shield fully collapsed as I closed in on the cabin. Blind fury descended over me as Daniel used a patio chair to smash through the French doors, while Stephen was forcing the lock on the front door with some kind of special tool.

With a roar, I hurled the man with all my strength in the general direction of the river and dove towards the house, as both men charged inside. Brianna's half-frightened, half-enraged scream chilled me to the bone. I landed on the porch just in time to see my mate swinging a long, wooden staff at Stephen with a superhuman speed and strength that forced him to back away as he tried to shelter himself from the relentless blows.

Daniel ran towards her, dart gun raised with his left hand, his right one rendered useless by a finger splint—the fracture no doubt resulting from our encounter at the Belvedere. I charged, slamming him into the wall. Seizing the opportunity off Brianna's momentary distraction upon seeing me, Stephen disarmed my mate before backhanding her. I roared once again, and raised my fist to crush Daniel's face just as something sharp stung my left side. My fist punched a hole through the brick wall by the fireplace as Daniel ducked, readying to shoot me again. I slammed my fist on his wrist, breaking it, and yanked out the dart embedded right above my hip. I cursed myself for not having turned my skin to stone again, but it would have made me too slow.

Ignoring the tingle slowly spreading through my right side, I bashed Daniel's head against the half-broken wall, cracking the back of his skull open. His eyes rolled back as he collapsed to the ground. Stephen's grunt of pain had my head snapping towards them. He shook his hand as if he'd hurt himself. Brianna threw a punch in his direction. He dodged and instinctively punched back, connecting solidly with her left cheek. The agent cried out and stumbled back, holding his wrist to his chest. My woman's head had barely jerked under the impact, her soft skin having taken the greyish tinge of stone, although not the full texture.

My beautiful mate!

With an angry scream akin to a war cry, Brianna threw herself at Stephen. He tried to push her away, but she swiped her hand towards his face. Instead of the retaliation I'd expected and had intended to intercept, Stephen stumbled back, his good hand flying to his neck. I watched with morbid fascination as his life's blood poured out of him. Snarling, Brianna leveled him with a hard, vicious stare. In that instant, she could have been channeling my dam—a true warrior goddess the enemy had been foolish to underestimate.

His eyes glazing over, Stephen fell to his knees before toppling to the side. As her adrenalin levels dropped, and the battle rage drained from her system, Brianna blinked and took a couple of steps away from her victim. Horror descended upon her features as she realized the finality of what she had done.

"You defended yourself, my mate," I said, fighting the fatigue which threatened to settle over me. "It was you or him. You didn't cause this. He did."

I came to stand in front of Stephen's corpse, breaking her line of sight. Brianna looked up at me, her body shaking. Drawing her into my embrace, I caressed my mate's hair, the soft skin of her cheeks—now back to normal—pressing against my chest.

"We must leave, my love," I said, my foggy mind racing as to where we could go. It would be another day before October 31st, but we couldn't stay here.

"They will send backup when they don't hear from them," she whispered.

"Yes."

Something in my voice had given me away. Brianna's

head jerked up, and she studied my face, a frown giving her gentle features a sterner expression.

"What's wrong?" she asked. Pulling away from me, she examined me from head to toe. "Are you hurt?"

"Not hurt, but one of the darts got me," I admitted reluctantly. "I don't know how long I can stay awake. I'm losing the battle. We need to get as far away from here as possible before I collapse."

Without a word, Brianna turned around and hurried to grab her bag, shoving into it what few items still mattered, mainly Khargal technology.

"They must have come by car," she said, running to the kitchen, pretending not to see the two corpses on the ground. "I can drive while you recover."

Brianna quickly packed a few things to eat while I rummaged through the men's pockets for the keys. Neither had them. I prayed to *Lar* that the man I'd tossed into the river didn't have them. Even if he'd landed in the water, the force of the impact would have likely knocked him out if not flat-out broken his bones. By now, he would have either sunk to the depths, or more likely been carried away by the current.

Our only hope rested on the two other men in the woods. As soon as Brianna finished donning her coat, I picked her up in my arms and flew to the first man I had slain. His broken neck would make for a far less gruesome sight than the one I had beheaded. To my relief, he had the keys. Considering the coldness of the night, the men wouldn't have parked too far away. Flying in the direction of the motion detector they had triggered, I surveyed the land, not daring to fly too high in case I crashed. The drug was weakening me way too quickly, and while I would survive the fall, my mate might not.

"There," Brianna said, after a minute airborne.

I didn't see it at first, my vision blurred from the effects of the drug, but flew blindly in the direction she pointed. As I closed the distance, I finally made out the outline of the dark vehicle. I'd never felt so vulnerable and useless, relying on my mate to look out for other potential enemies lurking nearby.

Just like all those years ago during my first flight, my wings suddenly gave up, wariness overwhelming me. Brianna screamed as we plummeted towards the ground. Holding on to her tightly, I managed to turn us around, landing on my back with a heavy thud, but transferring some of the momentum into a roll. We stopped less than gracefully nearly ten meters from the vehicle—which turned out to be some kind of minivan.

Brianna moaned in pain as she freed herself from my embrace. "Alkor! Are you okay?" she asked, pawing frantically at me in search of injuries.

I nodded, my head heavy and my back hurting. I didn't want to think what might have happened had we not already been descending to land.

"I must go retrieve the sensors," I slurred, wondering if I would have the strength to even get there.

"You're in no condition to fly anymore!" Brianna exclaimed. "Do they have Khargal technology?"

"No but—"

"Let's get you in the car."

"But—"

"Alkor, you're getting in the fucking car!" Brianna hissed in a tone that brooked no argument. "Who cares if anyone finds them? The Syndicate will certainly come clear out the corpses so the authorities don't come sniffing around their organization. If people find your sensors, they'll wonder what kind of paranoid freak had set them up, but it will not give them anything Earth shouldn't have. You can barely stand up, and more of those crazies could show up any minute. Get your ass in the van, right now."

The sensors didn't possess Khargal technology, but my design was far more advanced than what humans normally built. Still, the likelihood that the person who might discover them would be knowledgeable enough to realize it was slim to none. With much reluctance, I conceded defeat. Retracting my wings, I leaned heavily on Brianna who all but dragged me to the van with a strength she hadn't possessed a couple of weeks ago. I collapsed into the back of the van which contained some kind of cage, no doubt to contain me had the Rose Syndicate agents succeeded in their mission.

Sleep claimed me just as the vehicle started moving.

❧ 16 ❧

BRIANNA

I drove, blindly at first, content to follow the road away from the cabin and in the opposite direction from the waterdrome. But fearing I might be heading away from our rendezvous point, I stopped the vehicle long enough to use the onboard GPS. Based on its history, Stephen and his men had indeed come from the waterdrome. I hated not being able to see Alkor, lying in the back in his stone form, and not being able to pick his brain about our best course of action. And yet, a part of me loved that this time, I was the one saving him.

The van was not a rental. The cage setup at the back had taken a while to install, and the whole thing appeared custom —not some quickie job done at the last minute. I hadn't taken the time to check the license plate, but I didn't doubt for a moment that it would be altered or even a stolen one. I would also bet the Rose Syndicate had some kind of tracker on the vehicle. When Stephen and his goons failed to report in time, their acolytes would descend on us like a swarm of locusts.

Thinking of Stephen twisted my insides. I'd considered him a friend for so long. And even after what he'd done at the belvedere, I hadn't wished him harm. Why couldn't they have just left us alone? We weren't causing any harm. We just wanted to leave, go away in peace. And now… Now I had blood on my hands and a death on my conscience. Alkor had been right in calling it self-defense, but that didn't change the fact that this would haunt me probably for the rest of my days.

I stared down at my nails as that horrible scene replayed in my head. Something, some kind of primal instinct, had come over me. An exquisite pleasure-pain had coursed through my hand, a burning sensation at the tips of my fingers as my nails elongated by maybe half an inch, into sharp, pointy claws. With a mind of its own, my hand had slashed at his throat, removing the threat to my mate and to myself. Within moments of snapping out of that strange defensive trance, my nails had reverted to their normal length. My fingertips still throbbed, though it was no more than a dull, distant pain. In time, I would probably no longer feel pain when my claws came out or retracted, like Alkor's. In truth, I hoped there would never be any reason in the future for me to bring them out ever again. Well… maybe just to open an envelope or slice through the tape wrapping a package.

Shaking myself out of those somber thoughts, I decided to drive to the end of the road closest to the general direction of Gargoyle Ridge. In spite of that, we'd still have well over 100 km to cross by flight, if not more. Online maps didn't allow me to clearly calculate the distance between those two uncharted locations—or at least, I had no clue how to do it if such a feature existed. As we closed in on the road's end, I considered our options. With another twenty-four hour wait, no camping gear, and no proper shelter, this van could house us in relative comfort.

But the damn tracker...

There hadn't been a single residence in sight for a while now, although I had passed a few small dirt roads no doubt leading to hidden cabins in the woods. I'd been too frazzled to really pay attention to the name on the sign by the road, but this appeared to be some kind of fishing area. It hadn't begun snowing yet, probably wouldn't for another couple of weeks. I considered driving the van into the woods, rather than leaving it in plain sight in the empty parking lot, but that would draw more suspicions from the locals than leaving it here. Anyway, I expected us to be long gone before sunrise.

Turning off the engine, I stepped out of the vehicle, made my way to the back of the van, and sat down next to Alkor, still deep in stone sleep. I'd been driving for an hour and twenty minutes. By now, I suspected the Rose Syndicate had become aware of the mission's failure. The question was how close were the other agents? I prayed they weren't in the Northwest Territories, yet. There would be no available flights in the middle of the night, and driving would be even longer than just waiting for morning. But then, what if...

"I can almost hear you thinking," Alkor said, startling me.

"You're awake?" I asked, immediately feeling silly for the self-evident answer. His skin slowly reverted back to normal as he sat up, drawing me into his embrace. "Are you rested enough? The drug—"

"I am," Alkor said, reassuringly. "I woke every time you stopped the vehicle. As for the drug, Daniel only hit me with one dart. It would have taken at least a couple of them to fully knock me out. *Duramna* does wonders to eliminate toxins. How are you?"

"I'm fine. I'm… I'm really happy you're awake," I confessed, embarrassed to be so needy.

Alkor smiled and kissed my forehead. Stretching his neck, he looked out the window, probably to get a sense of where we were. He rose to his feet, hunched down so as not to bang his head on the roof, opened the side door of the van, and hopped outside. He looked slightly unsteady on his feet but not alarmingly so. Turning towards me, Alkor extended a hand to help me out of the vehicle.

Despite the crispness of the late fall night, I didn't feel cold. I should have been, but the air felt cool at best. Another blessing of Alkor's *dassa*. He flexed open his wings, stretching them while inhaling deeply. I stared in awe at his beautiful profile, his strong body, and beloved face. My savior, my mate, my incredible Khargal.

"The Syndicate will come for their van," Alkor said, matter-of-factly. "Are you still fine with the cold?"

I nodded. "Yes. I was just thinking about how wonderful it is that I hardly feel it."

"Good," he said with a relieved smile. "We could look for a vacant cabin to spend the next 24 hours, but we run the risk of them tracking us down. I'm sure we can find a natural cave in the mountains to shelter in until departure time. It is not the romantic last day I wanted to give you, but at least we'll be safe and out of reach."

"Actually, spending one day roughing it in the outdoors with my man sounds all kinds of romantic," I said, wrapping my arms around his waist.

"My beautiful *Hondassa*," Alkor said with a tenderness that melted my insides.

We kissed, his wings closing around us. For the next few minutes, we savored the moment before finally releasing each other.

Picking up one of the phones, Alkor called Lana to give her an update since once we flew from here, we probably wouldn't have a signal anymore. He seized the opportunity to ask her to use part of his estate to compensate the owner of the cabin for the damage the Syndicate had caused. That thoughtfulness only made me admire him even more.

After a last goodbye, where she wished us both well, he hung up, and I picked up our bag from the van. Although I worried about him and the lingering effects of the drug, Alkor reassured me he was fine before lifting off.

Although I'd never admit it, I'd been relieved that he preferred scouting for a place while carrying me rather than coming back for me once he'd found a place. I would have spent the whole time freaking out, seeing the boogeyman in every shadow, and hearing him in every sound.

As the wind whipped past us, the woods gave way to barren clearings, soon rising into rocky formations, and then mountains. It suddenly struck me that I hadn't felt the usual nausea triggered by my fear of heights. In fact, my only unease stemmed from concern for my mate who, admittedly, showed no sign of weakness whatsoever. He flapped his wings with strength and speed. According to him, we were flying at about 90 km per hour, and at least a hundred meters —or more—above the highest peak.

We flew for over an hour. Although I tried to convince Alkor to stop and rest, he plowed forward with unshakable determination, claiming to be fine. It eventually dawned on me that he already had a destination in mind. Sure enough, after well over ninety minutes of flight, he began circling around a specific peak, searching for a natural cave for us to shelter in. After a few misses, we finally found a decent-sized one, although it only looked like a tiny breach in the mountain face from the outside.

"You know where we are," I stated as we landed, dropping the bag that had grown heavy in my hands.

"Yes. This is Promontory Peak," Alkor said, cracking his neck and releasing the tension in his arms that had held me the entire time. "It's less than a fifteen minute flight from the pick-up point. Nothing can keep us from that rescue ship."

Tears welled in my eyes as the stress and fear that had been my constant companions for the past two weeks, finally gave way to relief.

"Thank you, God," I said throwing myself into Alkor's arms.

My ribs hurt a little when he embraced me, sore from his solid hold during the flight. As my head rested on his shoulder, exhaustion suddenly washed over me. My interrupted sleep was catching up with me at last. Sensing my weariness, Alkor lifted me into his arms and carried me to the driest section at the back of the cave. Despite the complete darkness, I could perfectly see the flat, elevated slab of rock upon which Alkor settled down. Lying on his back, he pulled me on top of him to spare me from the hard surface, and blanketed me with his wings.

Within seconds, my eyes closed, and sleep swept me away.

EPILOGUE

ALKOR

Under the clearest of blue skies and the bright rays of the sun, I laughed at my mate frolicking in the snow. She'd tried building a snowman, but the snow proved to be a little too powdery. Half of the snowballs she threw at me fell apart on launch, spraying her own face instead.

After sleeping almost until noon, Brianna had wolfed down part of the food she'd wisely brought for us. When I declined any and chowed down on some of the abundance of minerals and rocks surrounding us, her eyes nearly popped out of her head. When I reassured her that she'd likely not need to eat stones, despite my *dassa* coursing through her, she almost passed out with relief.

My mate was adorable.

While we had snowy regions on Duras, the harshness of the climates in those areas would rarely make it possible for her to enjoy such carefree play in this fluffy whiteness. To my relief, that news didn't distress her as Brianna had never been much of a fan of cold and snow. Nevertheless, she decided to make the most of this opportunity.

Night came and went without incident. And, at long last, the sun rose on the morning of October 31st. Brianna ate our remaining food, making me gulp down what few bits she couldn't swallow. Finally, we took flight, making slight detours on our way to the pick-up point so that we could admire one last time my mate's home world, and the planet that had sheltered me for the past millennium.

"Is that a Khargal?" Brianna asked, pointing at a dark form on the mountain ahead.

Just as I opened my mouth to answer, the form disappeared in a shower of sparkling lights. My heart soared, and I addressed a silent prayer of thanks to *Lar*.

"What...? What happened?" Brianna asked.

"My brother just got teleported to the rescue ship. You will meet him soon enough," I said, unable to hide the excitement in my voice.

As we completed our approach, a dark form in the distance with a long span of wings flew his way up, a precious human cargo in his arms. My throat tightened with emotion at the sight of another of my kin coming home with his *Hondassa*.

"Teleportation can feel strange," I said as we landed. "Do not fight it. I will be right there with you."

"Okay," Brianna said, eyes wide, her pulse racing in her neck.

No sooner had I spoken those words than the tingling sensation I hadn't felt in a thousand years spread through me as dancing lights surrounded my mate and me.

"Alkor," Brianna whispered, frightened.

Her hands tightened around mine, and then darkness swallowed us for less than a blink. Brianna's knees buckled as we reappeared on the transport pad. I caught her before she could hit the ground. Clinging to me, my mate fought back the nausea that twisted her stomach. Two Khargals stood before us, eyeing my mate with a tense curiosity. I frowned wondering what was going on.

Brianna straightened and inhaled deeply a couple of times, bringing the unpleasant effects of first time teleportation mostly under control. The Khargal to the right scrunched his face in displeasure while the one to the left beamed at my mate, clearly pleased. I realized then that the fools had made a bet she'd spill her guts all over the floor. Which meant another one of my rescued friends had already brought a human on board.

I bared my fangs at the two warriors to express my displeasure. They snapped to order, their eyes widening as they took in my seven horns and my uniform.

"Ma... Major?" the Khargal on the left asked, wiping his smile from his face.

"Drayvus," I said in a stern voice. "Major Alkor Drayvus of the VV Keav."

Funny how military discipline came back naturally even after all this time. I'd always been a bit of a stickler for protocol. Finding those two making bets at my female's expense while in the middle of a rescue mission had me itching with the urge to stab them with my wing spurs. Lucky for them they didn't report to me or I'd have them fly two dozen laps around the racing arena in stone skin. The fledglings would no doubt collapse from the weight in under two laps.

They saluted, suddenly nervous to have been found lacking in discipline.

"Welcome home, Major Drayvus," the no-longer-smiling Khargal warrior said. "Your dam and sire will greatly rejoice to have you safely returned. If you would kindly follow us, we will escort you to your quarters. At your earliest convenience, once you are rested and refreshed, Captain Traver will wish to meet you and…" his voice trailed off as he glanced at Brianna.

"And my *Hondassa*, *Fa* Brianna Brent," I completed for him.

Both men bowed their heads slightly in respect towards Brianna. Although she didn't understand their words, she returned the gesture with a nervous smile, accurately guessing they'd saluted her. The warrior retrieved a small device from his belt pouch and extended it to me. Although of a recent model, I recognized a universal translation device. My initial irritation with the undisciplined warrior almost fully melted. I nodded in gratitude and stored it in one of the pockets of my armor. As it sometimes caused slight headaches and dizziness on first use, I would wait until we'd reached our quarters before giving it to Brianna so she could fully understand the language of my people. The warrior gestured towards the exit before taking the lead. Wrapping my arm around my woman's waist, we followed in his wake, the second warrior trailing behind us.

Brianna's head jerked this way and that, her eyes wide as saucers as she took in her surroundings. The bright hallways, built tall and wide to accommodate a Khargal's size and height, curved at the edges and rippled along their length. It gave them an organic feel so different from the generally flat walls in human architecture. Unable to resist, my woman stretched out a hand and caressed the undulating texture.

"It's like a non-creepy, bright version of a Giger design," she whispered to me.

I didn't quite agree, but I could see some similarities if you significantly uncluttered his design and gave it a peaceful edge rather than his usual nightmarish visions.

We settled into the spacious cabin that had been assigned to me. Despite being a Major, these accommodations exceeded my rank. I didn't complain: my mate deserved nothing but the best. After a quick shower, Brianna laughed at me moaning when my taste buds practically had an orgasm at the first bite of Khargal food. One *gracking* thousand years without a taste of home. How had I not gone insane?

Although rather anticlimactic, the meeting with Captain Traver nonetheless gave me the greatest news: the war was over. That Brianna would need to adapt to our harsh world was enough without having to deal with the tensions of war as well. The not so great news: because of spatial distortion between Earth and Duras, while we'd been wasting away here for a thousand years, only twenty years had passed back home. This meant I was now physically a little over four hundred years older than my parents.

Bansial will never let me live it down.

In spite of that, thoughts of my young brother brought a smile to my face.

Reuniting with the two dozen other rescued Khargals, gathered in the common room of the ship, moved me to the core. I'd tried to keep in touch with as many of them as possible, but over the centuries, some had gone into deep *duramna* during my awake times only to rise after I'd gone into stasis myself. But seeing Tas warmed my heart the most. I'd feared he hadn't survived decades of captivity in the hands of the Rose Syndicate.

And yet, the most touching moment turned out to be my mate meeting the other handful of human females that had also chosen to come with their mates. Who would have thought a third of our surviving crew would have found their *Hondassa* on what my people continued to consider a primitive planet?

Although Captain Traver had mentioned the hero's welcome that awaited us back on Duras, nothing prepared us for the debauchery of fanfare the government officials lavished over us. How were we heroes? By surviving a crash and waiting a thousand years to be rescued while limiting the instances of trampling the Prime Directive? It quickly became clear that the government, having grown unpopular with the people, was using us as a PR stunt to revamp their image. I had no time for this.

After declining countless offers of honorific titles among the military, I all but fled the capital city to my sire's ancestral home: the Drayvus Aerie. Not all Khargals lived in aeries, many having elected to build their residences directly on the ground. Brianna feared she'd be trapped in the house without help to ferry her up and down. But I quickly reassured her that every aerie possessed a lift system to accommodate non-Khargal visitors or citizens, as well as elderlies or wounded Khargals temporarily—or permanently—deprived of flight capability.

My family had wisely elected not to come to the capital city for our arrival, or we would have been detained for days in the ongoing media circus rather than being allowed to enjoy our reunion in private. My chest constricted as my gaze landed on the sculpted façade of the aerie that had been my home for more than three hundred years. Carved directly into the mountain face, aeries were often designed to blend with the environment from a distance, the sculpting creating some kind of optical illusion.

My breath and pulse accelerated as the courtesy military shuttle began its descent over the landing pad at the back of the house. It sat a stone's throw away from the ledge my dam had kicked me from for my first flight so many centuries ago. Through the shuttle's windows, I stared at the tall, broad, and proud silhouettes of my approaching family, until they stopped at a safe distance. Brianna's hand slipped into mine and squeezed in a comforting gesture. Despite her own fears and insecurities, my mate was putting my own emotional turmoil and welfare first.

I didn't know what I had done to deserve her, but as long as I drew breath, not a day would go by that I wouldn't thank *Lar* for bringing her into my life.

"I love you, Brianna," I said, drawing her into my embrace. "You have melted this heart of stone and brought joy, purpose, and hope to my empty life. I promise to devote the rest of my days to making you happy."

Her eyes misted, and she gave me a trembling smile. "I love you, too, Alkor. You are so much more than I could have ever wished for. Thank you for giving us a chance to be together, in spite of everything."

Our kiss, tender and full of devotion, was quickly interrupted by the shuttle landing. Within seconds, the pilot, a young warrior named Tragan, hurried to the door and tapped on the wall interface next to it. The whistling sound of the ramp descending was soon followed by the hiss of the door sliding open.

"Welcome home, Major Drayvus and to you, *Fa* Brent."

I nodded distractedly, feeling slightly ashamed by my inability to properly thank the young soldier who had demonstrated exemplary discipline and adherence to protocol. But I only had eyes for my kin. Holding Brianna's hand, as much to comfort her as for my own need of support, I led her down the ramp to my waiting family. My dam hadn't aged a day. Her six horns, almost like a tiara on her head, gave her the same regal appearance I'd always attributed to her. But the vulnerable emotion on her usually stoic, battle maiden face, succeeded in breaking my neutral façade. Releasing Brianna's hand, I pulled my mother into my arms and gave her a crushing hug, which she returned in kind.

"My son," she whispered. "My firstborn son."

Tears pricked my eyes at the sound of the beloved voice I'd never thought to hear again. I retracted my wings as she closed hers around me. There was something special and unrivaled about the power of a mother's embrace that made you feel loved, cherished, and safe.

"We want a turn, too, female," my sire's rough voice said.

I didn't know how long Mother and I had held onto each other, but I didn't doubt it had drawn on longer than expected. With much reluctance, my dam released me. After one last caress over my horns and cheek, she stepped aside in favor of my sire. His embrace was rough and virile, as one would expect from an alpha male. But the excessive glistening of his eyes betrayed the depth of his emotions.

Sheira, my only sister, all but shoved my sire aside to get at me. He chuckled and shook his head with false despair.

She had fully matured into adulthood during my absence. Before a week had gone by, she'd definitely challenge me to a couple of sparring duels. Sheira always claimed she'd make General before me. Now that I was back, I looked forward to resuming that friendly competition. For now, though, I was too busy reveling in reconnecting with my *kher* and wiping the tears off her face. At a later date, I would make sure to remind her she'd wept with joy at my return.

When Sheira released me, Galtan, only a couple of years her elder, stood at a distance to give me a once over. I raised an eyebrow, wondering what that was about.

"You look old, big brother. Maybe we should call you great-sire now," he said in a mocking tone.

Cheeky brat.

"Whether great-sire or big brother, I still get to put you across my knees," I said, matter-of-factly. "Now get your scrawny tail over here and greet your elder properly."

He chuckled and, closing the distance between us, gave me the same manly embrace my sire had. He was the troublemaker of the family, and I looked forward to his antics.

Looking up beyond his shoulder, my wistful smile faded as my gaze locked with Marek, the second born. He stared at me with a mix of hurt, anger, and betrayal. Sensing my change in mood, Galtan released me from his embrace and took a step back to look at me questioningly. Noticing my stare, he followed my gaze to see what had prompted my reaction. Understanding dawned on his young face. With a sympathetic smile, he placed a hand on my shoulder, gave it an encouraging squeeze, and stepped aside.

Marek clenched his hands spasmodically, looking unsure

if he wanted to come to me or turn around and storm away. I carefully approached, stopping right in front of him.

"Hello, *bansial*," I said in a soft voice. He flinched at the pet name and scrunched his face, visibly fighting back tears determined to come pouring out. "I know it took me much longer than intended, but I came back, like I promised. Won't you welcome your brother home?"

I don't know which one of us reached for the other, but seconds later we held each other in a bruising hold like two Khargals drowning.

"Don't you ever *gracking* do that again," Marek mumbled, the facial bones along his jawline grating against mine as our cheeks pressed against each other's.

I chuckled. "I promise to tell the next sun I fly by to keep it's *gracking* flares to itself. I have better things to do than crashing on some planet so far away from home."

Releasing me, Marek punched my shoulder and whipped my thigh with his tail, giving it a nice sting.

"If you're done abusing me, I would like to introduce you all to my mate," I said walking back to my female who looked both moved and intimidated. "Mother, Father, *khers*, this is my *Hondassa*, Brianna. Brianna, this is my family."

They each took turns introducing themselves and embracing her. Although a little overwhelmed, Brianna's relief and joy at being so openly welcomed shone on her face. Since the death of her dam, she'd longed to belong to a family again. This was but one of the many things I intended to give her.

"You have brought me another daughter," Mother said to me while cupping Brianna's face in her hands. "Good, it is high time we start evening the numbers."

"Right, until you decide to kick her off the ledge," Sheira snickered.

Brianna's eyes bulged. "Your mother wouldn't do that. Right?" she asked, turning to my dam.

She gave my mate that wretched enigmatic smile that had so often traumatized me over the years, but amused me when it had been aimed at my *khers*.

"Who can tell the future?" Mother said mysteriously, a fiendish glimmer in her eyes. "Come on in, then. The meal will not eat itself. Welcome home, my son and daughter."

THE END

Ready for the next Khargal in the series? Check out STICKS AND STONES by Tamsin Ley!

When a mysterious man makes an offer on the life-sized gargoyle in Angie's garden, she quickly discovers her property holds more than sentimental heirlooms. Beneath its stony facade hides a world where legends are more than mythology, and ancient stories have roots from beyond the stars.

FROM THE AUTHOR

Did you enjoy a romance with a sexy alien gargoyle? Want to read more about hot, badass, alpha aliens that turn into marshmallows when they meet ***the one***?

Then you will want to read my <u>Veredian Chronicles</u> series where one courageous girl escaping slavery sets in motion a series of events that will change the fate of her people and that of an entire galaxy.

The Veredian Chronicles is the perfect read for fans of Nalini Singh and M.K. Eidem, pursuing their tradition of strong heroines, treacherous political intrigues, and the twists and turns you didn't see coming.

And because a picture speaks a thousand words, check out my cool book trailers!

Escaping Fate Book Trailer

Legion Book Trailer

Unfrozen Book Trailer

GLOSSARY

At-Ukris: aerial Duras animal. Looks like a cross between an eagle and an octopus roughly the size of a whale

Bansial: the Durassian word for sticky

Canikin: the Durassian word for lady parts

Dam: mother

Dassa: mating fluid

Duramna: stone form

Duras: Khargal home planet

Durassian: the Khargal language

Earthian: what Khargals call humans

Fa: the Durassian word for Mrs.

Grack: the Durassian expletive for fuck

Guurlk: Khargal liquor

Hondassa: Mate

Kher: Khargal term for siblings

Khargal: what gargoyles call themselves

Lar: the Durassian word for god

Macero: the Durassian expletive for hell

Maztek: Duras animal similar to an earth whale

Rose Syndicate: clandestine organization that is pursuing gargoyles and their technology

Sartek: a random predatory animal on Duras

Sigil: the device used for contacting the rescue beacon and teleporting to the rescue ship

Sire: father

Tanem: the Durassian word for temporary companion taken before a true mate

Want more sexy Khargals? Check out all the books in the series! You don't want to miss a single one!

https://nanceycummings.com/khargals-of-duras/

THE VEREDIAN CHRONICLES

Escaping Fate

Blind Fate

Raising Amalia

Twist of Fate

Hands of Fate

BRAXIANS

Anton's Grace

Ravik's Mercy

DARK TALES

Bluebeard's Curse

The Mistwalker

XIAN WARRIORS

Legion

Raven

Bane

THE SHADOW REALMS

Dark Swan

VALOS OF SONHADRA

Unfrozen

Iced

ABOUT REGINE

Regine Abel is a fantasy, paranormal and sci-fi junky. Anything with a bit of magic, a touch of the unusual, and a lot of romance will have her jumping for joy. Hot alien warriors meeting no-nonsense, kick-ass heroine give her warm fuzzies. Through her Veredian Chronicles series, Regine will take you to an exciting alien world full of mystery, action, passion and new beginnings. Follow Amalia and her Veredian sisters as they fight for their freedom and the right to love.

When not writing or reading, Regine surrenders to the other passion in her life: video games! As a professional Game Designer and Creative Director, her career has led her from her home in Canada to the US and various countries in Europe and Asia.

Facebook
https://www.facebook.com/regine.abel.author/

Website
https://regineabel.com

Regine's Rebels Reader Group
https://www.facebook.com/groups/184551832176494/

Newsletter

http://smarturl.it/RA_Newsletter

Goodreads

https://www.goodreads.com/author/show/
16289162.Regine_Abel

Bookbub

https://www.bookbub.com/profile/regine-abel

Amazon

https://www.amazon.com/Regine-Abel/e/B06W2MTBRV/